NO REST
FOR THE RESTLESS

OTHER WESTERN TITLES BY R. W. STONE

Trail Hand (2006)
Badman's Pass (2016)
Across the Río Bravo (2017)
Canadian Red (2018)
Only the Stubborn Survive (2019)

NO REST
FOR THE RESTLESS

R. W. Stone

BLACK
STONE
PUBLISHING

Published in 2022 by Blackstone Publishing

Printed in the United States of America

ISBN 978-1-0940-8642-2
Fiction/Westerns

Version 1

CIP data for this book is available
from the Library of Congress

Blackstone Publishing
31 Mistletoe Rd.
Ashland, OR 97520

www.BlackstonePublishing.com

Dedicated to Dr. Rafael C. Cedeño Terrades.
No man could ask for a more loving and supportive brother.

"The man of principle never forgets what he is,
because of what others are."

—Baltasar Gracián

CHAPTER ONE

Flames from burning twigs and branches flickered in the night air, silhouetting the ten men sitting around the campfire. Some were drinking what remained of a pot of weak coffee, a couple were still chewing on the remnants of the hardtack, and the rest kept themselves busy cleaning their weapons.

The group's leader was the notorious Fred Morris, who, together with Bloody Bill Anderson and George M. Todd, had been one of William Clarke Quantrill's top lieutenants in the bushwhackers, or Quantrill's Raiders as they came to be known. He had been present at the infamous Lawrence, Kansas raid in 1863.

"So what's the plan, Fred?" one of the men asked, kicking an ember back into the fire ring. He was a short, dark-haired sort who sported a large hat with one side of the brim pinned up to the crown. He carried a Starr arms revolver stuck crosswise in the front of his belt and had been with the group for going on five years.

"The bank opens at nine," Morris explained, "and for about an hour, they're busy. I reckon on us hitting it around ten thirty." He paused to look into the faces of the others. "Here's what we're going to do," he continued. "We'll split into two groups outside of town and then ride in slow and easylike from opposite directions, east and west. We'll meet near the bank, but spread out. Don't want to draw attention to ourselves. Nelson and you, Jake"—he flicked his head in their direction—"will take up positions outside, where I want you to watch the horses; then, once we're inside, keep your eyes peeled for any sign of the law. The rest go in the bank with me. I figure they won't put up a fight, so once we get the money, we ride south in three separate groups like bats out of hell."

"Where and when do we meet to divide up the money?" asked Craig, the youngest member of the gang. He was a thin man who sported two belt knives and a Remington revolver in a well-worn holster. He also wore stovepipe chaps.

Morris was visibly bothered. "Don't trust me all of a sudden, Craig? Maybe you're afraid you're going to be cut out of a fair share?"

The man looked alarmed. "No, Fred, it's not that."

"What then?" Morris pursued. "Have I ever stiffed any of you?"

"Sorry, boss. I trust you. It was a stupid question," Craig said sheepishly.

"Damned right it was," Fred replied angrily. "You'll all get your share when I'm good and ready. Any problems with that?" His eyes traveled the circle.

The men stirred uncomfortably. Most said nothing, just shook their heads, while a couple muttered a response.

"That's more like it," Morris said. He rolled a cigarette skillfully as he looked around, his eyes settling on Nelson. "You go stand guard now," he told him. "I'll have Blake spell you around midnight."

Patrick Nelson had not been in Morris's gang long, having joined up only about a month earlier. He had explained to the gang leader that he had been on the run for a while. His family had been killed, one and all, in the war, and that he was fleeing the law after a foiled stagecoach robbery, during which he had been identified by a passenger.

At first, Morris had been a little suspicious of the newcomer, but when Nelson showed him a wanted poster, it helped convince the leader of the truth of his story.

Since then, Nelson had proved to be a man who worked tirelessly around camp and followed orders with little or no complaining. The fact that he was hell on earth with his fists didn't exactly endear him to the other men in the gang, but it did impress their leader.

"Right, just let me finish this coffee," Nelson muttered. He was of stocky build, with a bull neck and a flat nose. A small scar ran over his right eye that gave the impression he was not someone to tangle with.

"Finish it quick, and then get out there," Morris snapped, wanting to dissuade a couple of the men from their opinion that the boss favored Nelson in spite of the fact that he had just joined the band of guerrillas.

Nelson took a final swig and tossed the tin cup down near the fire. "Yeah, yeah, Fred, I'm on my way." He adjusted his holster, picked up a Sharps carbine, and then faded off into the darkness.

Nelson covered the ground quickly over to a stand of large, old oak trees. He could still see the flickering of the fire, but he was no longer close enough to hear what the men were saying. A disadvantage if they were talking about him.

About five minutes had passed when he heard a rustle in a clump of bushes to his right.

"That you, Captain?" he whispered, trying to visually penetrate the inky blackness around him.

"It is," came back a voice, and again a slight rustling. "And

I've been damned uncomfortable surrounded by vines trying to attach themselves to me and being eaten up by bugs. So, is it still on for tomorrow?"

"Yeah. Around ten thirty," Nelson whispered, his head turning back every few seconds to make sure he wasn't being watched. He continued: "They'll be ten of us. I'm to remain outside with Jake Ward and keep watch for any sign of the law and to guard the horses while the other eight are inside."

"Good work. And don't you worry, we'll be there," the voice said. "Just make sure those horses aren't anywhere close by once they enter the bank."

"I will," Nelson whispered hoarsely, anxious to end his time with the gang, for he was tired of sleeping on the ground and eating beans twice a day, only occasionally supplemented with meat from a potshot one of the men made.

"Take care of yourself, Pat," the voice said, and then all was quiet again.

"Don't I always?" Nelson replied to the night, as he stared into the woods, trying to catch a glimpse of his boss. Then he turned and took a few steps over so he could lean against the trunk of an oak. He wanted to make sure McKenzie hadn't been spotted by any of Morris's gang.

At midnight, he was relieved of his guard duty as promised. Nelson promptly returned to the camp where he collapsed into his bedroll. And despite his saddle being a poor excuse for a pillow, he was fast asleep within a couple of minutes.

* * * * *

After a quick breakfast of reheated rock-hard biscuits and greasy beans, nine of Morris's men saddled their horses and quietly rode out of camp. The sun was shining brightly for the first time in over a week. When the outlaws were less than half a mile from town, they split up into two groups. Nelson and four others headed out and around the town in order to enter from the west, while the five remaining riders, which included Fred Morris, waited a half hour before continuing on into town from the east.

With the end of the Civil War not that far in the past, the majority of small towns in this part of the West were made up largely of veterans and their families. As was to be expected, the average home had at least one firearm, but usually there were more. Most veterans had already been experienced hunters before signing up, but, once they did, even more practice often made them deadly shots. The women—young, old, single, married, widowed—had taught themselves how to shoot to both feed and defend themselves, as well as others, while their men were away fighting. Morris knew all too well that to charge into such a town, whooping and shooting up the place to scare the populace into submission, would no longer work. It was more likely that they would retaliate.

For this raid, Morris planned to arrive in town both quietly and cautiously, and while riding in, to be assessing the possibility of opposition. He had instructed his men that there was to be no shooting the town, unless they were met with resistance from the bank employees, and then only at his say-so.

It wasn't that he was adverse to the idea of violence. Quite the contrary. Morris had proved that fact time and time again while riding with Quantrill. But now he was a little older and, he hoped, a little wiser, having seen Quantrill and Bloody Bill Anderson hunted down like dogs. This time his idea was to go in slowly and get out quickly, before anyone in town could retaliate.

The two groups of outlaws arrived at the town limits a little after ten, as planned. They held back there and then slowly started filtering in by ones and twos. By ten thirty all of Morris's men had gathered near the bank. As instructed, Nelson and Jake were stationed around the corner outside the bank, keeping an eye on the horses. Of the two, Jake was the nervous one. He couldn't keep still and kept looking around anxiously.

"Don't be such a nervous Nellie," Nelson said. "Relax, or you'll give us all away. Here, you take the reins, and, if it will make you feel better, I'll cover you if any shooting starts. That make you feel any better, Jake?"

Nelson wasn't sure it would calm Jake, but he handed him the reins of two horses before walking over to his own horse, where he pulled out a Henry .44-caliber rimfire rifle from the saddle scabbard. He preferred its lever action, and the tubular magazine would give him more firepower, if needed, than a Sharps single-action carbine would. In the meantime, Jake had his hands full with the reins of four horses. The other six were loosely tethered to the hitchrack.

Several minutes later, Nelson watched as the last of the gang filtered into the bank; then he waited for the count of ten before turning to Ward and whispering behind his back: "Hey!"

When Jake turned around to face him, Nelson clouted him squarely on the jaw with the rifle butt, knocking him unconscious instantly. He didn't bother gathering up the horses' reins, just swatted one of the four on the rump, causing him to run off with the other three trailing close behind. He moved over to the hitching rack, releasing the remaining six horses. They took off after the others, heading north and away from the town.

Nelson ran back to the corner of the building and positioned himself behind a barrel, with his rifle aimed at the door of the bank. He knew what was going to happen inside, but he was determined to be ready in case something went wrong.

Patrick Nelson noticed several lawmen sneaking toward the bank. He waved them down once they were in easy range.

They settled across the street, opposite the bank. One of the men nodded an acknowledgment at Nelson.

* * * * *

Inside the bank, the robbers fanned out upon entering, with Morris standing front and center, waiting to have the full attention of everyone in the bank. He waited, now thinking about the fact that there had been very few people out and about when they rode into town. It had meant nothing then. But even though he was feeling confident when he walked in, because things had been going smoothly, suddenly he began to wonder why there had been so few people out. He pushed the thought aside and focused on the occupants of the bank, pleased to see only one customer—a tall, well-built but slender man, wearing a white suit complete with vest and a round, flat-crowned hat. He held a walking stick in his left hand, and Morris couldn't help but admire its shiny and ornate silver ball handle. Morris looked around, noting the four bank tellers stationed at five foot intervals behind the iron-grated windows, just as he had expected.

He stood there a full minute before he drew his Navy Colt .36-caliber revolver calmly, holding it level, and announced: "This is a stickup! Don't move unless I tell you to. I'm not afraid to use a gun, and neither are my men."

He looked from one teller to another. He believed he saw fear in their eyes as they glanced at each other.

"Excuse me, sir. Would you mind if I ask a question?" the one customer asked.

Morris turned his head to study the man whose manner appeared to be both calm and polite.

"What does a city dude like you wanna know from me?" Morris asked somewhat hesitantly, having been thrown off guard by the tall man speaking up in the middle of a robbery. "Make it quick," he said brusquely, in an attempt to get the upper hand again.

The tall man nodded. "I'll be quick, I assure you. I was just wondering if you have ever heard of the Pinkerton National Detective Agency?"

At the mention of that name, several of the robbers looked over at Morris with concern, each familiar with the stories surrounding its founder, Allan Pinkerton, who had successfully uncovered and stopped a first plot to kill then President-elect Abraham Lincoln.

"Haven't most folks?" Morris replied. "What of it?"

"Well, I thought I'd better warn you that those fine gentleman there behind the windows . . . the ones acting as tellers . . . are actually Pinkertons. Except for that fellow in the middle, that is. He's the town's sheriff."

At that announcement, the tellers pulled up double-barreled, express-style shotguns and leveled them directly at Morris. The Pinkertons knew that nothing, but nothing, strikes more fear into anyone than the sight of a twelve-gauge shotgun pointed right at your middle. Especially when cocked.

"Allow me to introduce myself," the man in the white suit continued, still as cool as can be, his blue eyes never leaving Morris. "I am Agent John McKenzie in charge of this investigation, and you and your men are under arrest. Now before any of you try to do anything foolish, I would also like to inform you that there are a dozen or so sheriff's deputies stationed outside, as well as a few more Pinks." McKenzie stopped, pulled out his pocket watch, and glanced at it before continuing. "I assure you that any chance for escape has passed . . . Your horses are loose, last seen heading out of town."

The men to Morris's right and left began trading looks of

either fear or defeat, but they always came back to the tall man in the white suit. Having avoided looking at Morris, they slowly and carefully lowered their weapons, placed them on the floor, and took a step back as they raised their hands high in the air.

Morris, however, was still thinking things over, trying to come up with a new plan. He knew that given his life of crime, a term in jail would not be anywhere near as likely as the hangman's noose. But when his men put down their weapons, he knew their chance of going down fighting had evaporated.

John McKenzie had worried about Fred Morris since he and a select few others had begun planning the takedown of the outlaw and his gang. He knew perfectly well that there was no predicting how a mad dog will react, especially once it's cornered, so he watched Morris closely and spoke very softly. He pegged Morris as the kind to be willing to risk it all.

"Not the time or the place, Morris. Don't be a fool," he cautioned.

The fact that they knew his name made Morris come to a decision quickly, however, McKenzie noticed the outlaw's thumb inch back as he started to cock his Colt revolver. In a move so fast it was difficult to follow, the man in the white suit shifted forward, pulled a long hidden blade, almost a sword, out from inside his cane, and brought it down on Morris, hard. The razor-sharp blade cut deeply into Morris's forearm, the thug's tendons almost severed in a few places. Unable to hold onto his weapon, Morris was forced to drop it to the floor.

As Morris stood there, helpless and in pain, McKenzie pointed the tip of the sword at the far end of the room. "All right, everyone up against the wall . . . Keep your hands held high. I'm assuming I don't have to remind you that a twelve-gauge can cut a man in half when the range is close . . . like this."

The members of the gang didn't need to be told twice. They

were halfway across the room before McKenzie finished what he was saying.

After working his way over to the door and opening it, McKenzie shouted, "Pat, you out there?"

"Sure am, sir, so are the others," Patrick Nelson replied, but then added for the benefit of the robbers: "No man will get out of there without us seeing . . . and killing . . . him!"

The next five minutes seemed to pass slowly for the men outside. But then the front door opened. John McKenzie emerged first, followed by the sheriff, then a line of eight outlaws in handcuffs, and four Pinkerton agents, all with double-barreled shotguns fixed on the robbers.

Patrick Nelson stood up and rested his rifle against the nearest wall. "Nicely done, sir," he said to McKenzie, who by now had resheathed his weapon into the shaft of the cane.

"Couldn't have done it without all your hard work, Pat. Rest assured, I'm going to make sure Allan hears of this." McKenzie was referring to Allan Pinkerton.

The sheriff walked over to McKenzie and patted him on the shoulder. "I sure have to hand it to you," he said, a broad grin on his face. "I'll admit that wasn't how I would have played it, but you have to give credit where credit is due. Things worked out this time, and I'm much obliged. Especially since none of my men were hurt and the money remains safe."

McKenzie told the sheriff the Pinkerton office would be contacting him, then he stepped back and tipped his flat-brimmed hat. "Sheriff, it was good working with you and your men. Believe me, no one is more pleased than I that we got Morris and his cohorts. Appreciate your cooperation in their capture."

The detective reached into his pocket and pulled out his briar pipe and tobacco pouch as he watched the nine men being lead off to the jail. When the pipe was filled, he brought a match to it, creating a billowing cloud of smoke. When the smoke had dissipated, he noticed that Nelson had taken out a cigar, so he struck another match and held it out for him.

"Now if you will excuse us, Sheriff," McKenzie said, returning the matches to his pocket.

McKenzie's preparing to leave reminded the sheriff of something. As the two Pinkerton men began to walk away after a final handshake with the sheriff, the lawman reached into his vest pocket.

"No, wait a moment! Damn, I almost forgot! This came in on the telegraph early this morning, and what with all the commotion . . . preparing for the arrival of Morris's gang and all . . . it plumb slipped my mind. It's for you." The sheriff pushed the paper at McKenzie.

"Thanks, Sheriff," the Pinkerton man said as he unfolded the missive.

When he was done reading, he turned to Nelson, his voice serious when he spoke. "It's from Allan. Seems like we have ourselves another assignment.

"Another already?" Nelson said, weariness making his face look haggard.

"I'm afraid so," McKenzie replied. "Must be an important one too. Allan used the word urgent twice."

Nelson sighed and shrugged. "Seems like getting a few beers and a good night's sleep is out of the question now."

"Seems so, but let's go find out when we can get the next train out of here," McKenzie said. "We're headed to St. Louis."

As they walked, Nelson blurted out, "That fake wanted poster you came up with sure was a stroke of genius. I don't think Morris would have trusted me without it. Hell, the rest of his men didn't."

"I can't take the credit for that idea," McKenzie said. "Harry came up with it. You've got to hand it to him . . . that man is just full of clever ideas and tricks, even if he is a bit of a scoundrel."

Nelson didn't say anything as he thought about Harry Howser, an amusing con man, who McKenzie had brought in on a number of cases.

The two bought tickets, but learned they had enough time before the train left to have a beer or two.

Sitting at a table at a nearby saloon, McKenzie said: "You know, Pat, I've got to say there's nobody I'd rather work with or have at my side in a fix than you. Truthfully."

"Goes for me too, sir," Nelson said in response.

"Pat, the war's over, there's no need to 'sir' me anymore. You know that, right?" McKenzie asked, wiping the beer foam from his lips with the back of his hand.

"Yes, sir," Nelson replied.

CHAPTER TWO

It was around eight o'clock in the evening when David and Marianne Holt led their child to bed. They stood next to their nine-year-old son, Andy, as he knelt down at the side of his bed and prepared to say his nighttime prayers.

"Now I lay me down to sleep, I pray the Lord my soul to keep. If I die before I wake, I pray the Lord my soul to take," the boy recited.

"Very good, son," Andy's father said. "Now, young man, give your father a great big kiss and then climb into that big comfy bed so your mother can tuck you in."

After the boy had snuggled down under the covers, his mother lovingly pulled them up tightly around her son's small shoulders.

"Now, Andy, I know this is not your usual bed, but as long as we are here visiting Gramps, this hotel is where we will be staying," she explained. "I know it's different from being in your own room at home, but your father and I will be right on the other side of that door should you need anything."

"It's all right, Mother," Andy said bravely. He was trying

not to appear as frightened by the strange surroundings as he really was.

The boy's father sensed his son's fear, so he sat on the edge of the bed and reassuringly rubbed Andy's arm, saying: "Your mother is right. You don't have anything to worry about. We're right through that door there . . . oh, maybe twenty feet. We'll be able to hear your every move." He patted Andy's arm and then stood up. "And that nice soldier who played hide-and-seek with you is right outside that door there." He pointed to the door that led into the hallway. "Gramps had him put here to protect us. Nothing can bother you while you sleep, I promise you."

"Papa, why is that soldier protecting us?" the boy asked.

"Well, son, you know your grandfather is a very important man in the government. I've told you he's a real army general. That's all it is," David told his son before kissing him on the cheek and squeezing his arm.

Then Marianne bent over and gave her son a kiss on his forehead. "Goodnight, my love," she said. "Sleep tight. See you in the morning."

As they started to leave the room, Andy spoke up. "Would you keep that lamp lit, please?"

David smiled. "Sure thing, tiger. Anything for our little boy."

"I'm not that little anymore," Andy said.

"No, no you're not, my love," Marianne said and blew him a kiss.

* * * * *

The night was so peaceful and uneventful that outside the door in the hotel's hallway, the army corporal assigned as the family's bodyguard had a hard time just trying to stay alert.

The Holts had thoughtfully moved a comfortable chair out

from Andy's room for the soldier to rest in, but he ignored it, afraid he might drift off if he sat down. And there was no way the corporal would allow himself to fall asleep on duty. Not this time. Only once had Corporal Alvin Jones seen what his sergeant did to slackers in their outfit, and that had been enough to put the fear of God in him.

Fortunately for the corporal, one of the hotel's night staff, who introduced herself as Clara, brought him a large pot of hot coffee around midnight to help him stay awake. It was hot and strong, but by two o'clock in the morning, in spite of several more cups of the java, the soldier decided he would sit for fifteen minutes. Very soon thereafter, in spite of fighting off the desire, he nodded off to sleep in the comfortable chair.

* * * * *

It was seven the next morning when the corporal was jarred awake by several loud screams coming from the room he had been guarding. Jumping up from the chair on wobbly legs, his heart pounding, Corporal Jones reached for the doorknob to the room, but the door was locked. As the screams seemed to be intensifying, Jones drew his pistol and kicked the door open with all the force he could muster.

Splinters went flying, and as the door flew open, the corporal quickly leveled his handgun and surveyed the room. He saw that the boy's mother, near collapse, was being held up by her husband as she sobbed into his shoulder. The pair were standing next to the boy's bed, but there wasn't a trace of little Andy anywhere to be found.

Corporal Jones quickly ran over to the boy's bedroom window, which he found locked from the inside. On this floor of the hotel, the rooms had big windows with a view of the city, but there were no balconies. Even so, just to be sure, he opened the window to look out. It was a five-story drop, straight down.

The soldier then ran into the bedroom next door, but again there was no trace of the boy. The door to the hallway in Andy's parents' room was also locked from the inside, as were the windows.

"Oh, my God," Marianne sobbed. "Andy! My little Andy!"

The boy had vanished from the suite.

CHAPTER THREE

Senator Carl Schurz paced nervously back and forth behind a large oak desk in his office at the *Westliche Post* newspaper, of which he was a full partner with Emil Pretorius. The former brigadier general had recently moved to Missouri from Detroit, where he became editor and joint proprietor of the periodical. Then, within a year, he was elected to the senate.

Standing across from him was Allan Pinkerton, head of the largest privately owned detective agency in the country. He stood quietly, waiting to be filled in, to learn the specifics of the summons which seemed to be clouded in mystery thus far. He was concerned by the distraught behavior of the senator.

Finally, after a lengthy pause, the senator turned to face him, clearing his throat as he did so.

"Mr. Pinkerton, let us dispense with the formalities, shall we?"

"Certainly, Senator," he replied. "As you wish."

"Thank you," Schurz said quietly. "I have called you here to discuss a problem that is most troublesome to my family, and therefore, by extension, to myself, our government, and our nation. Personally, it is the most worrisome of news I can ever remember."

"How can we be of assistance, sir?" Allan Pinkerton asked, still uncertain as to why he had been called in by Schurz and how it would involve the Pinkertons. Genuine curiosity was obvious in his voice.

The senator filled him in on the background and then reached over and picked up an envelope from his desk. He opened it and took out a letter which he then shook open and studied silently. Looking up, he once again cleared his throat.

"To be brief, this letter explains that my nine-year-old grandson Andrew . . . we call him Andy . . . has been kidnapped."

"I didn't know you had a grandson, sir," Pinkerton slipped in.

"Marianne, his mother, spent a lot of time with us when we lived in Wisconsin. She lived with her aunt and uncle who really had no interest in raising her, even though she had no one after her parents died. So my wife took Marianne under her wing when she was about eight. We both grew to love her very much. She lived with us on and off until she met David, married, and had a child. When Andrew was born, she asked us to be both Andy's godparents and grandparents."

After a pause that stretched on uncomfortably, Pinkerton asked: "And that is the ransom letter?"

The senator replied with a nod of his head. "I'm afraid they are requesting a rather substantial sum of money," he stated. "They say here in this letter that either I pay this ransom . . . or they will kill Andy." Schurz slapped the letter in anger.

"Allan, I know of your loyal service to our late President Lincoln, and I'm well aware that you protected Lincoln with your life. I also know that you protected his family faithfully during the war."

"I deeply regret we weren't there to stop that fanatic Booth, sir," Pinkerton said sincerely.

Senator Schurz nodded his head. "We all do. Nevertheless,

I need to know whether or not your agency has the ability to handle something of this nature?"

The detective pondered the gravity of the situation for a moment before answering. "Senator, we have handled abductions in the past. Some with more success than others. This situation is not that unusual . . . although the amount of money being demanded is steep. What is different here and what makes it problematic is that we are dealing with the abduction of a child. That plus the potential for horrific ramifications. Have you considered bringing in the US Marshals?"

Carl Schurz shook his head. "US Marshals are too independent a group . . . very individualistic. They're usually called in to replace or support local law enforcement. My understanding, however, is that your agency is especially well-known for its confidential intelligence operations."

Pinkerton suppressed a smile. "That is most kind of you to say, but, again, might I ask, sir, what about the army? After all, you are a general."

"This letter is very explicit about what will happen if I am caught trying to track down these monsters . . . or if an attempt is made to rescue the boy," Schurz explained. "And though it's just a gut feeling, I fear if we call in the army, Andy's kidnapping will be common knowledge all over the state and beyond within a short time. My experience in politics and the newspaper business only serves to reinforce my beliefs. Therefore, before I risk exposing Andy to even more harm, I want your opinion here and your help."

Pinkerton nodded. "Well, first off, I don't believe this is some loner, Senator. Something like this would take far too much planning, and the idea of one man pulling this off all by himself would be foolhardy." The Pinkerton cleared his throat. "Sir, before I accept this job, I'd like to introduce you to one of my best operatives. Since I didn't know the reason for our meeting, I brought him along in case a field assignment might be involved. He is waiting right outside."

"Excellent," Schurz nodded. "Shows good thinking on your part. Please, show him in."

Pinkerton walked to the door, opened it, and ushered in a tall, lean man near middle age with short hair, a pencil-thin mustache, and a clearly military demeanor. As an ex-military man himself, the senator quickly judged him to be a former officer, due to the way he carried himself, his air of confidence, and his calm but serious manner in his present surroundings.

The man walked with a slight limp, the result of a musket ball that hit his thigh during the War with Mexico. The limp was barely perceptible except to the most astute observer, but, even so, it was enough to end his career in the Marine Corps. As a marine officer, John McKenzie had always led from the front. After his injury, even though he most certainly would have been allowed to continue on with a staff position, that was not in his nature. If he was not able to outrun and outperform the men he led into battle, he would just as soon retire, which is precisely what he did.

The ex-marine was impeccably dressed in a dark suit. A carnation was attached to his coat lapel. He carried a black cane with an engraved silver knob. Upon entering the room, he immediately removed his flat-brimmed hat and held it in what the military would refer to as an "at ease" position.

Senator Schurz couldn't help but notice the man's penetrating stare. It was as though the man's eyes didn't want to miss a thing. The senator also suspected that many a woman would find those piercing blue eyes of his most appealing.

"Senator Schurz, I would like to introduce Captain John McKenzie, ex-marine," Pinkerton said. "One of our best field agents."

The politician walked around his desk, and once he stood in front of McKenzie, he extended his hand, saying over his shoulder to Pinkerton as he did so: "Allan, you should know there is no such thing as an 'ex' marine." He then looked back at Captain McKenzie. "Pleased to meet you, sir."

"I know of you from your contribution in the war, sir," McKenzie replied. "I assure you, the honor is all mine, Senator. How might I be of assistance?"

"Mr. Pinkerton is deciding on how best to help me in the matter of a child kidnapping," Schurz informed him.

McKenzie nodded, showing no reaction. "I understand, and since we are here, I assume it must be high up the chain."

"Plenty high, I'm afraid," Allan Pinkerton inserted.

McKenzie glanced over at his boss with obvious surprise. He turned back when the senator motioned for the two men to take a seat in chairs across the room. He followed them over and took a seat himself.

He looked McKenzie in the eye, saying: "Andy is my grandson. He was taken a day and a half ago from a hotel right here in St. Louis. These people, these lowlifes, have no regard for the sanctity of human life and no empathy for the heart of a mother or father. The kidnappers want me to pay a fortune to get Andy back . . . or the bastards will kill him. A little nine-year-old boy!" He pushed himself off the chair and went over to his desk where he again picked up the ransom letter, his face turning a bright red from his rising anger.

"With all due respect, sir, could I request that you put the letter down and not touch it again," McKenzie said firmly.

"What? Why?" the senator asked, irritated at being told what to do.

"There's a lot of new thinking in our line of work," McKenzie explained as he leaned forward in the chair. "We look for clues now much more carefully, because we know the criminal always leaves behind clues to his identity, even if that means only minuscule bits. I believe it to be true, having conducted many investigations. In fact, the agency once solved a case based solely on a smear of food found on an envelope that eventually led us to the guilty party."

"Really?" Calm now, the senator was intrigued.

"I know someone who specializes in precisely such small details and clues," McKenzie said. "He is currently teaching at the university here in the city. I would like him to look at the letter . . . and the envelope it came in . . . to see if it contains any evidence. So . . . the less the letter is handled, the better."

Senator Schurz thought over what he had just been told, then said: "Captain McKenzie, I'm sure you realize this whole matter must remain completely confidential."

"I understand completely, sir, and I assure you that we can be entrusted to keep the matter confidential."

"Now, Captain . . . you too, Allan . . . who are the *we* you keep referring to?"

"The team I plan on putting together for this assignment. There are three men I have in mind, based on the nature of the crime. I have worked with all of them in the past, and I believe they are all the best at what they do."

Schurz cocked his eyebrow at the ex-marine and looked at Pinkerton, who nodded his head at the senator. "So, including the scientist you mentioned . . . that's four more people who will know. That's getting to be quite a number of people to involve in this matter. It appears I must remind you again what the ransom note says . . . that if there is even a hint of the police or others being involved, Andy will die."

"Nonetheless, sir, I trust each and every one of the people I would use on the case," McKenzie said.

Schurz sat thinking before he stood up from his desk chair where he had settled and said: "Very well, Captain McKenzie. What choice do I have but to trust to your judgment?" The politician looked out the window for a minute, before walking over to the chairs again and sitting down.

"This is not to be repeated outside of this room, gentlemen," Schurz said very softly, "but the president has told me that you have the full authority of his office to do anything it takes to resolve this issue, because we can never allow the families of politicians to become the targets of crazy or evil men or political fanatics again. However, there is one caveat. Nothing you do, legal or otherwise, must ever come back to reflect negatively on this office, or that of our president. Understood?"

"Yes, sir. Understood. I believe we are thinking along the same lines," McKenzie assured the senator. He then turned to face Allan Pinkerton. "Boss, we are taking this case, right?"

"It looks like it. Yes."

"In that case, I quit. You'll have my letter of resignation on your desk by morning," McKenzie said, staring his boss square in the eye.

"What?" the other two men said almost in unison.

McKenzie remained silent until his boss's expression of shock finally changed to one of understanding.

Pinkerton nodded his head and began explaining to the senator: "Sir, in detective work it pays to avoid repercussions, especially political or legal ones. This way, if something happens as a result of any of McKenzie's team's actions . . . meaning McKenzie . . . something that you or I do not wish for, or approve of . . . well then, we simply cannot be blamed."

McKenzie added with a sarcastic grin: "Right, I'm a free agent, if you will."

Senator Schurz relaxed as he pursed his lips and let out a

loud sigh. He turned back to face the two men. "Of course. I see that now. Very clever. Very clever, indeed."

"Then if . . . or rather when . . . we are successful, I can take my job back. Perhaps even get a raise," McKenzie added jokingly.

"Hey, John, let's not get carried away here," Pinkerton said.

"Allan, if this man pulls this off and gets my grandson home, I'll pay his damned salary for a year," the senator replied emphatically as he patted his pockets.

"There is one thing more we'll need, sir," McKenzie added.

"And that is?" the senator asked.

"We need to know whether or not your grandson is still alive," McKenzie replied.

"I . . . I don't understand. Surely he's still alive," Schurz said, almost collapsing into his chair, looking as though the possibility that he might not be had never crossed his mind until now. "How would I have any proof?"

"I realize this isn't something that you want to contemplate, but there have been kidnapping cases where the person taken is . . . well, doesn't survive . . . and this isn't learned until after the ransom is paid. I know these are things you don't even want to think about, but . . ." McKenzie said, his hesitation growing as he watched the look on Schurz's face turn to something akin to horror.

"I don't even have two weeks to gather the funds, even if I had the money. But you're saying . . . Andy may already be . . ." Schurz couldn't bring himself to say the last word.

McKenzie nodded. "That's why we need definitive proof that Andy is still alive." McKenzie walked over to the desk and used a pen to turn the letter so he could read it. "It says if you need to communicate with them, you can respond through the ad section of your newspaper.

"So, here's what we will do to verify that Andy is alive. Allan will help you write your response to the ransom letter today, which needs to be kept brief. You will demand that the kidnappers provide you with a photo of the boy, looking as healthy as the day they took him, which was two days ago. It must be a photo . . . we don't want them sending us a fin—" McKenzie stopped abruptly when he realized he had said too much.

The senator gasped in horror. "You mean . . .?"

"Sorry, sir," McKenzie said with sincerity. "Despite their threatening tone, we don't know that these people are in fact killers. Nonetheless, they have abducted a child from the family of a United States senator, so we must take them very seriously. And until we have more information or a motive, we must be careful. And Allan, have them deliver the photo to the newspaper."

"Couldn't we catch them here then when they deliver it?" the senator asked. "Then we could force them to take us . . ."

McKenzie put his hand up to stop Schurz from imagining the possibility of a simple way to get Andy back. "They will know to take precautions. Most likely they will use someone they don't even know to deliver the photo or some response. Probably someone down on their luck who'll do it for half a dollar and the promise of a drink. Someone, in other words, unaware of what he is delivering and why."

While McKenzie was talking, he kept glancing at the newspaper on the table in front of him. A slight smile came to his face, because it had given him an idea.

"Because we don't know if Andy is still in St. Louis, or even Missouri," McKenzie began, "we will demand a photo of Andy holding a newspaper with the current date showing. Tell them that only then will you begin to work on their demands. Inform them that however they choose to deliver the photograph is acceptable to you, since how the abductors choose to do so is irrelevant to our investigation. What is important to us will be the photograph of the boy holding the daily newspaper."

The senator nodded again. "All right. Allan, I would like to get this demand ready for the newspaper right away, as I need to get out to the ranch to be with my family. The ad will run in the paper tomorrow"

"Give me ten minutes while I walk Captain McKenzie out," Pinkerton responded, "then I'll be right back.

McKenzie shook the senator's hand.

"One last thing, John, before you leave," said Pinkerton, "since I want you both to hear this. It occurs to me that since the Secret Service specializes in counterfeiting, I think they would be the best ones to analyze that abduction letter and envelope. After all, paper and ink identification is one of the areas of expertise. If anyone can tell us anything about the paper and where it came from, they can. I can drop it off today with your permission, Senator."

"I still find it hard to believe they're able to learn things from a piece paper," Senator Schurz muttered.

"Following paper trails is what they were created to do," said McKenzie.

"Allan, if I have anything to say about it," Schurz said, "you shall have the full support of the Secret Service in this. I'll stop by their office on the way to the ranch."

"Thank you," Pinkerton replied. "I'll be back in ten minutes." Then, he and McKenzie left the office.

CHAPTER FOUR

"How was the trip getting here?" Pinkerton asked.

"It was touch and go for a while . . . almost missed the train to St. Louis. But we made it. I forgot to tell you Pat Nelson is with me. He did some really fine work with the Morris gang. He's waiting downstairs."

The two friends had first met when Nelson had served under McKenzie in the Marines. John considered him the best hand-to-hand combat instructor and bare-knuckle fighter he had ever seen. Nelson had gotten his training at a young age, when he worked his way up at a boxing club in Chicago from janitor to sparring partner, even if his pay didn't reflect it. For that reason, Pat, as he was called by everyone, began participating in unauthorized back-street, bare-knuckle fights. He soon became a local legend, but, after breaking his nose a couple of times, as well as his cheekbone on another occasion, Pat decided there had to be a better way to make a living. The need to overcome his limited education and scant resources, coupled with a burning desire to better himself, led him to the Marine Corps. And, after a couple of years in the corps, Nelson's physical fitness and fighting skills led him to win promotion to corporal in charge of his company's hand-to-hand-combat instruction.

He saw action in the Mexican War where he saved Captain John McKenzie's life when he single-handedly turned back a twenty-man bayonet rush with his musket, pistol, and sword. It wasn't the only time.

After that war, both retired from the corps, and when Captain McKenzie was offered a position by Allan Pinkerton, the first man he requested to join him as a field agent was Sergeant Patrick Nelson.

"Hello, Allan, what's the job this time, sir?" Nelson asked and stood up to shake Pinkerton's hand.

"Kidnapping of a child," Pinkerton replied.

Nelson tipped his small Stetson hat back and whistled. "Damn. As far as I'm concerned, anyone who'd do that . . . you know . . . hurt a kid . . . is about as low as they get."

McKenzie nodded, still thinking about what he had learned as he fired up his briar.

"I'm not going back to Chicago until this is over. In the meantime, you two have my complete support on this, so anything you need to solve this case, let me know," Pinkerton said, letting his words fade away before he brought up the subject he had been thinking about. "John, besides the young scientist you mentioned, who else do you have in mind for your team?"

"Harry Howser for one," McKenzie replied quickly.

Howser was another one of John McKenzie's group of special acquaintances who he kept in his back pocket when he needed specialized skills on a case. Harry had worked on three Pinkerton cases before, so Nelson was familiar with him as well. Officially, Harry was listed as an independent contractor to the detective agency, but unofficially, in his free time, he was a part-time con man, pickpocket, and prestidigitator extraordinaire. McKenzie knew him to be loyal to the right causes and a trusted friend, who had come to his rescue when he was about to get pounded up, or worse, by a group of drunks outside a hotel in New Orleans. He had been wearing his uniform. They shared a drink afterward and managed to see each other once or twice a year when McKenzie wasn't on a case.

Then, a year or so later, after McKenzie learned more about his craft as a magician and the tricks he was able to do, he convinced Allan that he would be useful on certain cases, in spite of Harry's checkered background. Pinkerton went to bat for him, and eventually the paperwork went through, and Harry got his badge.

"So me, you, and Howser . . . that makes three of us," Nelson said. "Anyone else?"

"Might I point out that having a woman on the team might give you more options," Pinkerton suggested. "How about Alicia?"

The beautiful Alicia Faye had been one of the South's most favorite entertainers. Her singing, dancing, and acting were so legendary below the Mason-Dixon Line that it wasn't long before she was dubbed the Queen of the South. She had spent the war years traveling all over the Confederacy entertaining, but secretly, however, Alicia was a Union loyalist spy and one of Allan Pinkerton's most trusted agents.

At the mere mention of her name, McKenzie had felt a tightness in his chest, so at first he was reluctant to agree, for John had been in love with Alicia for a long time.

"And don't forget, she and Harry go way back, though I admit she's more experienced in this line of work than Harry will ever be," Nelson said.

McKenzie had unconsciously flushed at the mention of the friendship between Alicia and Harry that had developed over the years. So when Nelson looked from Allan to McKenzie, he saw the look on the latter's face and regretted his words.

"Her work for me during the war was exemplary, John," Pinkerton agreed, trying somehow to get McKenzie to at least weigh in on the subject.

The ex-marine captain nodded his head as the other two seemed to be staring him down.

"A woman on the team does have certain advantages," Pinkerton reiterated, wrinkles appearing across his forehead as he tried to figure out McKenzie's resistance to the idea.

What would it be like to see her again? McKenzie was thinking to himself when Pinkerton stepped up closer.

"John, I have to admit I'm worried," Allan said seriously. "The agency's head . . . *my* head is on the chopping block here. I promised Schurz we could handle this when, bloody hell, we don't even know where to start looking."

"Well, I very much doubt they're hiding in northern Maine," Nelson inserted in the pause.

"Very funny, Pat," Pinkerton commented, his irritation showing.

"Listen, I know you're both worried. I am too," McKenzie was finally talking. "It may feel like we're standing over an abyss, but we've already learned something."

Pinkerton frowned. "What's that?"

"Someone in the group speaks German, since they want to correspond through his paper which is in German."

"Or they know someone who is fluent in the language," Pinkerton suggested.

"And another thing," McKenzie continued, since they had gotten off the subject of Alicia, "we will learn the whereabouts of the boy from the kidnappers themselves, and they probably won't even be aware they're doing it."

"I don't follow," Pinkerton admitted. "Tell me fast, I've got to go back and get our demand ready."

The three men walked down the stairs of the building located at Fifth and Market. McKenzie stopped at one of the desks to pick up the latest edition of a newspaper. Then he turned back to Allan and Pat.

"Allan, as we've said, we don't even know where Andy is, so this is where the photo will answer that question for us." McKenzie held the newspaper up. "It includes everything we need to know. The place and the date."

Pinkerton laughed aloud and felt like shouting. "The name of the newspaper will tell us where they are! Of course! That's brilliant, John."

"So, what do you think the odds are that when the senator's demand is made," McKenzie asked, "these people will be smart enough or devious enough to go out of state to another city to get a daily newspaper in order to fool us?"

Pinkerton was still smiling when he replied, "That would never happen. They'll go right over to the nearest corner, grab one . . . just like you did."

"And if they won't meet the demand?" Pat asked.

"Then we still won't know where Andy is," McKenzie admitted. "But I'm betting they're so hungry for the money, they won't be thinking, and they'll meet our demand."

"If you're right, you might just be worth that raise, after all," Allan Pinkerton joked.

"Thanks, but, hell's bells, Allan, we both know you'll just bill it to the client."

Allan Pinkerton thought for a moment, then smiled. "You know, that's not a bad idea," he said.

"One more thing," McKenzie said.

"What would that be, John?"

"We need to get a guard or two over at the hotel where the Holts were staying. It's the kidnapping scene, and since it's where I intend to start our investigation, I'll need it sealed off so no one can go snooping around or cleaning up."

"That's already been done," Pinkerton assured him. "But I'll confirm it."

McKenzie turned to Nelson. "Pat, I want you to check out the train station, see if anybody remembers seeing the boy. Also find out where someone could take a child . . . I don't know . . . a children's home, orphanage . . . Also, check with the police to see if they can put you in touch with anybody who knows the gossip going around the city. If they want to know what you're working on . . . make something up."

"So what's your first move?" Pat asked McKenzie.

"First thing in the morning, I'm going over to the university," McKenzie replied.

"To meet with Professor Piper, I'm assuming?" Pinkerton asked.

"Right. Jimmy the Wunderkind," McKenzie joked. "I'll need him for a couple of things."

"The know-it-all kid, you mean," Nelson muttered under his breath. He didn't mind Jimmy, and he appreciated his intelligence, but sometimes he came off a bit too cocky.

"I'll expect updates on the progress you make," Pinkerton reminded the agents as they neared the front doors. "I'm sure Senator Schurz will want to be updated as well, and he'll be coming to me for any scrap of news."

When Pinkerton reached the door, McKenzie said, "We shouldn't be seen together in public if we can avoid it, but I'll be in touch with you as I learn things, as long as I'm sure we aren't jeopardizing the boy."

"Understood," Pinkerton said. "Good luck."

* * * * *

Later that afternoon McKenzie walked down the street to the nearest telegraph office where he sent off two messages. Both of them said the same thing:

> Papa needs you desperately. The family is in deep trouble. Come home to St. Louis as quickly as possible. Will expect you by midnight.

The wording was a simple prearranged code. The "family" obviously referred to the Pinkertons. "Papa" was McKenzie, and "home" meant the local headquarters of the Pinkerton agency in whatever city was mentioned. In this case, St. Louis, a city that would be the fourth largest in the country in ten years' time. The last line was a reference to the Cinderella story they used when time was of the essence—"midnight" meaning as fast as humanly possible, which didn't give Harry Howser or Alicia Faye much time to get to Missouri. But he knew that neither was far from St. Louis at the present time, because they both kept him updated on their whereabouts so they could be contacted quickly if needed.

* * * * *

Next, the marine-captain-turned-detective checked into a hotel suite, figuring his team of detectives would use it as their headquarters. He booked it for one week, even though he thought that was being optimistic. Once he settled in, he ordered room service, but once it arrived, he just nibbled at it. He smoked his pipe for nearly an hour, thinking, and then wrote up his notes before taking a bath and shaving, trying to get rid of that gritty feel from traveling. He went to bed right before ten and was sound asleep before one of the city's clocks chimed the hour.

The next morning McKenzie dressed and went downstairs, where he had his usual breakfast of black coffee, one fried egg over-easy, and a single slice of lightly buttered toast. When he left the hotel, he headed to the nearest livery to acquire a horse.

He chose a large bay gelding that looked to have both stamina and a calm disposition. Although many livery horses are often old and worn-out, McKenzie was impressed with this beauty. The ride to the university down streets punctuated by large trees casting long August shadows was pleasant, almost relaxing.

After securing his mount to a hitch rail at the side of the university building which housed Piper's office and workroom, McKenzie climbed the stairs to the second floor. The sign on the door read: J. PIPER, HEAD, DEPARTMENT OF MINES AND METALLURGY.

Professor James Piper actually was, in fact, a child prodigy. By the age of sixteen, he was already a Doctor of Science and Philosophy. During the war, Captain McKenzie had worked with the boy, who was able to analyze different gunpowder samples in an attempt to locate powder barrels that had been stolen from a Union armory. To say that at the time McKenzie had been astounded by Jimmy Piper's medical and scientific abilities would be an understatement.

McKenzie respected Jimmy and his work, and for that reason he knocked, not wanting to barge right in.

"Enter!" Jimmy, the scientist, called out in response.

McKenzie inched open the door to find Jimmy Piper bent over a small flame, his back to the former marine. The room smelled of sulfur, chlorine, and several other chemicals which made McKenzie turn up his nose and want to breathe through his mouth.

"Jimmy, how are you?" McKenzie asked.

The young academician turned around, delight spreading over his face when he saw McKenzie. He nearly knocked over a beaker as he swiveled around. He pulled off his glasses and rushed over to grab McKenzie in a bear hug that caused the ex-marine to stammer at the exaggerated show of affection.

"Enough, lad, enough," he managed to say as he stepped back, smiling uncomfortably as he looked at Jimmy. "It's good to see you too. It's been a while."

"Yeah, it has. But what brings Captain John McKenzie to the halls of academe and the lab of one Professor James Piper?" Jimmy asked eagerly, hoping this meant work in the area of detecting.

"Well, I thought you might like to see a little of the world that exists outside this room, and at the same time help your country."

The scientist's eyebrows arched up. "Really? Help my country . . . you mean it? Sounds intriguing. So, just how would I . . . or we . . . go about doing that?" he asked.

"Let's go sit down," McKenzie said, pointing to a small, beat-up table with two chairs sitting over by the covered window. "Before I even begin, I need you to know that what I am about to tell doesn't go beyond these walls. Don't mean it to sound so cloak-and-dagger, but nothing I tell you, whether you take on the job or not, can be divulged to anyone ever."

Even though Jimmy knew McKenzie was dead serious, his enthusiasm couldn't be contained. "So tell me, John!"

"I need you word . . ." McKenzie insisted.

"I promise," Piper said and put his hand over his heart. "You have my word . . . Now tell me."

After an explanation of what McKenzie knew so far about the kidnapping of Andy Holt, he outlined what he needed from Jimmy.

"We'll be going over to the hotel where the kidnapping occurred once Harry Howser gets here. Pat Nelson came to St. Louis with me. I'm hoping you can put some of this science of yours to good use." McKenzie reached into his coat pocket and removed a piece of paper.

"In the meantime, here are my notes on what we know so far," John said, handing over the paper, "which isn't much, as you can see. I wrote them up last night, and it's essentially what we just discussed. I didn't include any names intentionally. Oh . . . I almost forgot. I'll need you to bring that rolling laboratory of yours to the hotel," McKenzie added. "Be there at eight o'clock sharp."

Jimmy nodded in agreement. On a whim, and without even asking permission, the chemistry wunderkind had purchased, with university funds, of course, a huge used steamer trunk, complete with compartments and drawers inside as though it had been designed especially for his needs. He took it to one of his friends who made a few changes, adding a base and wheels to it and converting it into a sort of portable science laboratory.

"After that, once we're through at the hotel, maybe you could swing by the local offices of the Secret Service. They will have had the ransom letter and envelope for less than twenty-four hours, but you never know. Just flash that Pinkerton badge I gave you a while back . . . it should get you in. You still have it, don't you?" McKenzie said.

Jimmy nodded, even though he thought it was a ridiculous question.

"Well, if that doesn't do the trick, then show them this." McKenzie produced a letter from another pocket and handed it to the young man. "Allan had the senator write these up before he left town for his ranch, and they were delivered to me at the hotel shortly after I checked in."

Jimmy skimmed the letter and whistled softly upon finishing. "Signed by General . . . oh, wait, he's senator now . . . Senator Schurz no less! That ought to do the trick."

"Use it only as a last resort, son," McKenzie ordered. "The more people aware that something is going on, the more danger that boy could be in."

"I understand," Jimmy replied. "You can count on me, Captain. I give you my word."

"I wouldn't be here if I didn't already know that, Jimmy" McKenzie said, and with that he left the university.

CHAPTER FIVE

As soon as McKenzie left the university, he rode over to Benton Barracks, again enjoying both the ride and the way the horse stretched out his legs once they were away from the city. Once there, he learned that the soldier, Corporal Alvin Jones, who had been guarding the senator's grandson, was currently being interviewed.

Given his former status in the Marines, along with references from the Pinkertons, it wasn't hard for him to be granted permission to observe the interview. The time spent was well worth it, because it gave him time to study the soldier, as well as to gather preliminary information about the goings-on the night the boy was taken direct from the horse's mouth, so to speak.

When the interview finished, McKenzie headed for the Pinkerton offices, leaving the gelding at the back of the building and entering through the door in the alley. He went to the office that was always available to out-of-town agents when they were working on a case in St. Louis. He spent the rest of the day there, scribbling notes, committing to paper everything that Corporal Jones had said. It also made him aware of just how little they knew, and it was already day four.

From time to time, he left his desk to pace the room, tonight biting on the stem of his pipe instead of smoking it. He stopped to stand in front of two large maps—one of Missouri and one of St. Louis. A map of the country hung on the opposite wall. He was studying the state and local maps, with which he was less familiar, hoping that Andy's kidnappers had not taken him far. It was McKenzie's father who had instilled a love of maps in him, but far from being the only thing, and as a child he could get lost in them for hours. But right now, even the maps couldn't hold his attention. He wanted to go over to the hotel and check out that boy's room before potential evidence was destroyed.

It was dark out when he finally left the Pinkerton building for his hotel suite.

* * * * *

Early the next morning, McKenzie ate breakfast in the hotel dining room, during which he gulped down three cups of strong coffee that he figured he needed after a restless night. Then he rode the horse over to headquarters.

By the time he arrived, he started feeling ready for the day, even excited, knowing Harry and Alicia were arriving tonight at the latest, though they weren't traveling together. So when McKenzie opened his office door and entered, he was not surprised to find a man sitting at his desk, wearing a seersucker suit and looking comfortable. He had set his brown derby hat on the top of his desk to the right.

"Nice to see you again, Harry," McKenzie almost shouted. "Now get your damned feet off my desk!"

Harry Howser smiled, slid his feet to the floor, extending his hand out as he arose. "Nice to see you too, boss."

"Knowing you as well as I do" McKenzie said, shrugging

out of his coat and placing his hat on the coat tree kept at the side of the door, "I assume you've already gone through my desk drawers. Find anything interesting?"

Harry grinned. "Just some notes about a recent kidnapping. I presume that's why you're currently in need of my very specialized talents?"

McKenzie shook his head in disbelief, chuckling, but then his expression quickly turned serious. "Harry, I do need you, but more importantly, a little boy needs us all. This one's very important."

"Sure, anything for you, John, but we've handled a few kidnappings before. Why is this one so important?"

"It goes way up toward the top," McKenzie explained.

"The boy's related to Allan Pinkerton?" Harry asked, his eyebrows shooting up in surprise.

"No, but just as important," McKenzie said. "Ever hear of a man named Schurz?"

Harry scratched his head. "The same Schurz who was a general at Gettysburg and then became a newspaper man? Wait a minute, Carl Schurz is the one who was recently elected . . ."

McKenzie nodded and interrupted Harry to say: "The very same one. It is Carl Schurz's grandchild that has been kidnapped." He didn't feel it was necessary to explain the actual relationship of Schurz and the boy.

The con man whistled and shook his head. "I've seen some high-stakes rackets and some very clever stings in my day, but this one takes the cake. Abducting the grandson of a sitting United States senator. Damn, that's risky! So why not just pay them? Surely Schurz has got the money . . ." He hesitated, before adding: "He does, doesn't he? Wait, just how much are they asking?"

"That's just it, Harry. They're asking for more money than even he can raise," McKenzie replied.

Harry frowned. "What then?"

"I guess these people . . . whoever they are . . . think he can get it out of the newspaper or that the government will pay for it somehow."

"They're crazy! No way. It'll never happen," Howser exclaimed. "We may be out of luck on this one, John."

McKenzie stared at Harry for a good half minute before saying: "You want to tell that to the senator? Or maybe you'd prefer to talk to the boy's mother and father?"

"No, no thanks," Harry said, shaking his head. "I get it." He thought for a moment. "So where do we start? And where do I come in?"

"For now, take these notes and read through them," McKenzie said, picking up several pieces of papers and handing them to Harry.

"Who else have you got working on the case?" the magician asked.

"Jimmy and Pat, and we're still waiting on Alicia, who should be arriving tonight. In the meantime, we'll check out the hotel where the family was staying when the boy was taken. We'll meet in an hour and a half."

McKenzie wrote an address on a small piece of paper and handed it to Howser. "The professor will be there with us to lend a helping hand."

Harry smiled broadly. "How is Jimmy, the little egghead?" he asked. "Still as skinny as a flamingo?"

"Same as always. Makes me feel old just looking at him," McKenzie replied honestly.

"Face it, pal," Harry said jokingly. "We're both old, but at least I've maintained my boyish good looks and charm."

McKenzie grinned. "Like all magicians, that's just an illusion, isn't it? Or maybe in your case . . . a delusion. But you go on believing it."

* * * * *

Twenty minutes later McKenzie headed over to the hotel to talk to the person in charge before Harry and Jimmy arrived.

Upon his arrival, he asked for the manager. A small balding man, perhaps in his fifties, holding his pince-nez, came out of a back office behind the front desk and politely introduced himself.

"My name is Samuel Kirkland, sir. I am the hotel manager. How might I be of service?" he asked.

"Is there some place we can go to speak privately?" McKenzie asked. He leaned forward and opened his palm slightly to reveal a Pinkerton National Agency badge.

To his credit, the manager did not seem surprised or act as if McKenzie's visit there was anything out of the ordinary.

"Most assuredly, sir. Through that door over there, please. I will meet you on the other side and escort you to my office."

McKenzie barely took a step into the office before he stopped. The walls of the room were covered in animal heads, and as he glanced from one to the next, the eyes seemed to be looking right at him.

"My brother's handiwork," Kirkland explained to McKenzie, who figured he had gotten into the habit with anybody who entered. "Most everybody has the same reaction you did. But you get used to them.

McKenzie, keeping his eyes off the walls, introduced himself again before taking a seat. He started out slow, asking Kirkland only general questions.

"A terrible thing," Kirkland said, his head bobbing. "Nothing like this has ever happened here before. Our entire staff is quite shaken."

"I'm sure they are. Now from what I understand, a soldier had been stationed to guard the family."

"Yes, sir, that is correct," Kirkland said, fidgeting in his seat under the questioning.

"Do you know anything about him?" McKenzie asked.

"Matter of fact, I know of Corporal Jones," Kirkland offered. "His family lives here in St. Louis. I would say the young man is above suspicion. He's a career soldier, won a medal for bravery at the battle at Fredericksburg. His older brother Samuel . . . he wasn't so lucky. He was killed at the Battle of Second Manassas."

"The family has remained loyal to the Union, then?" McKenzie asked. "Do you think there could be any grievances between the Jones and the Schurz families?"

"I would never doubt the Jones's loyalty to the Union," Kirkland said adamantly. "As for any animosity toward Schurz . . . he hasn't been in Missouri that long . . . since right after the war. How could anyone really have any problem with him? German fellow, he is . . . Schurz, I mean."

"Yes, I know," McKenzie murmured before continuing on. "What about any financial problems the Joneses might have had over the years?" he asked patiently, remembering he was talking to a hotel manager, not a criminal.

"His brother left a tidy sum of money to Alvin specifically, from what I heard," Kirkland said. "But I couldn't say for sure that there are no financial issues within the family. You'll have to talk to someone else about that matter. Quite frankly, it is none of my business."

Although McKenzie knew not to rule anyone out this early into an investigation, in the case of Alvin Jones, especially after listening to Kirkland, the lead detective felt the corporal wasn't a likely suspect in the commitment of the kidnapping. He sat thinking before shifting his questioning to the night of the incident and the morning of its discovery.

"Mr. Kirkland, could you tell me if anything out of the ordinary happened that night, or even leading up to it? Especially concerning the cleaning lady who brought the corporal coffee that night.

"We call them housekeepers," Kirkland informed him before he answered the question. "Coffee? I'm confused. What time did this occur, if I might ask?" The manager seemed perplexed by McKenzie's question.

McKenzie checked his notes quickly. "According to what we have learned, it was around midnight that a member of your staff . . . a woman . . . brought a pot of coffee to Jones. She said she had heard that he was up on that floor, so she had come up with a pot of coffee, saying she thought it might help him stay awake." He tapped the paper for emphasis.

"I'm afraid what you've just told me is all out of the ordinary," Kirkland said as he removed a small handkerchief from his jacket pocket and wiped his brow nervously.

"How is that?" McKenzie asked. Now it was his turn to be perplexed. "Why is that unusual?"

"Well, first of all, Mr. Schurz asked that the floor his family members were to stay on be emptied of other guests, if possible . . . and that night there were no other guests on that floor. We made sure of it. We also never have staff clean rooms at night, unless we are short on rooms and need to ready them for new arrivals. That wasn't the case in this instance. And, besides that, we have a strict policy against housekeepers handling food or drinks of any kind . . . they're not to touch them. So you can understand my confusion. The person who gave the coffee to Jones isn't in our employ, couldn't have been a member of our cleaning staff. Anything having to do with food is assigned to kitchen and room service staff." Kirkland shrugged and sat silently for a number of seconds before asking: "Do you have a name . . . or perhaps a description of this woman . . . the housekeeper in question?"

"The soldier described her as having brunette hair . . . wears spectacles. She was thought to be in her late thirties to early forties, light complexion, somewhat portly. Nothing to distinguish her other than a prominent mole on her right cheek . . . near the corner of her lip. Jones thought she said her name was Clara."

Kirkland was becoming agitated the longer McKenzie continued to talk. "Detective McKenzie, there is not a woman who works here who fits that description. There clearly must be some mistake."

John McKenzie shook his head. "I'm afraid it's not a mistake. Jones was very certain about his description of the event, particularly about the woman." He paused to scratch his head for a moment. *It appears we now have the first piece of information about a potential suspect*, the former marine thought to himself. *This woman was brought in specifically for the job, confirming what we had been thinking all along: This was a well-laid out plan to abduct the boy.*

Kirkland gasped after sitting quietly for some time. "Good God, you mean someone infiltrated our staff and impersonated a hotel worker in order to abduct the child?"

McKenzie nodded. "Mr. Kirkland, I suspect that if this woman didn't actually perform the abduction herself, she certainly must have assisted others in perpetrating the crime."

"Please, I beg you," the hotel manager said passionately. "Do not let this become known publicly. It could ruin our long-standing reputation for both security and privacy."

"Don't worry, Mr. Kirkland," McKenzie said. "For any number of reasons, our conversation will remain confidential, I assure you. However, truthfully speaking, I am more interested in recovering the boy than I am in protecting your hotel's reputation."

Well after the Pinkerton detective had excused himself and left the office, Samuel Kirkland remained slumped over his desk, staring at a wide-eyed wapiti hanging above the door while McKenzie waited for the others to arrive by the front desk.

CHAPTER SIX

By eight o'clock, John McKenzie, Harry Howser, Jimmy Piper, and Samuel Kirkland all stood in the fifth floor hallway in front of the hotel room from which Andy Holt had been abducted. The damaged door had been locked, even though anyone could have gotten in easily by reaching through the damaged door panel, so after Kirkland unlocked the door, McKenzie politely thanked and dismissed him. He also dismissed the guard, telling him to check back in a couple of hours. As the guard turned to leave, Corporal Alvin Jones arrived, responding to a request McKenzie had made to his superior the day before, when he was at the army base.

It was fortuitous, since the first thing the detective wanted done was to confirm with Jones that nothing had been moved, and that things, especially the chair, were still in the same place as they had been that night.

"I don't understand it, sir," Corporal Alvin Jones said, while staring into the room. "I never left my post . . . not for one minute."

"And you saw no one in the hallway the whole time you

were on guard . . . with the sole exception of the hotel maid . . . the housekeeper . . . that is," McKenzie confirmed.

"That's correct, sir, and she did nothing that raised my suspicion. She was quite friendly. We chatted for several minutes. Then that's about the last thing I remember before I heard screaming coming from the boy's room early in the morning. When I tried the door to the boy's room, it was locked, and because I could tell that the screaming was coming from that room, I kicked it in. The boy's parents were standing near his bed, but the bed was empty, and there was simply no sign of Andy whatsoever. The lad was gone."

"Yet you clearly saw the boy in his room with his parents the night before?" Harry Howser asked.

"I did. In fact, after the boy was ready for bed, I watched as Mr. and Mrs. Holt tucked him in and said goodnight. Mr. Holt stepped over to the door, thanked me, then closed and locked the door. I heard it," the corporal said, nodding to himself as he recalled details from that night. "The next morning when I broke into the room, I checked the doors and windows. They were locked from the inside. But . . ." He hesitated. ". . . even sealed up tight like that, the boy had vanished."

"I'm sorry to have to ask you this, Corporal Jones," Jimmy said, moving closer "but it was reported to me that you do admit to falling asleep for a short time out in the hallway, correct?"

The question clearly upset the soldier. "That's what I don't understand. I had at least three cups of black coffee . . . never had stronger in my life . . . to help me stay awake. And that is what doesn't make any sense. I've stayed up for far longer shifts than this without falling asleep. Not a one." Corporal Jones stopped for a time as if he were suddenly deep in thought before he added with a shake of his head: "Now though . . . after this . . . the first chance my sergeant has to get me alone, I'll be a goner.

I heard the request for this guard duty came from the sarge's old general, Schurz himself. They served together at Gettysburg."

"From one military man to another, Corporal, let me take care of that for you," McKenzie said, trying to reassure the distraught soldier and hoping he could keep Jones out of trouble.

"And this cleaning lady you mentioned, she was the one who brought you that coffee?" Jimmy asked, injecting himself in the conversation.

"That's right. The first time I saw her, she was pushing a cart. I figured she was collecting dirty linen. She nodded at me and then moved on down the hall a ways . . ." Jones indicated the place by walking down the hall. "About here, I guess . . ."

McKenzie cut him off to ask: "Do you remember what time that was?"

"Not long before midnight . . . maybe a quarter of," the corporal replied. "We spoke for a moment . . . mostly about having to work long nights." Again he paused, and then he snapped his fingers and said: "She called it the cemetery . . . no, that wasn't it . . . Graveyard . . . that's it! The graveyard shift. Now, mind you, I didn't know what that meant. She said it's a term used by some miners. So then . . . let's see . . . about a half an hour later, she came back . . . I figured she needed to get her cart . . . but she was kind enough to bring me a whole pot of hot coffee."

"Did either of you suggest coffee before she left the first time, Corporal?" Jimmy Piper asked.

The corporal seemed surprised at the question. He scratched his chin. "Well, now that you mention it . . . she did bring it up when we were first talking. She suggested for these long nights, I should always bring along some, because it would help me get through the night. It didn't dawn on me that she would actually bring me a pot, but I was very grateful when she did."

"Did you add anything to the pot? A wee bit of the Irish, maybe?" asked Harry Howser. "You know . . . Who-Hit-John . . . Red eye?"

"Absolutely not. On my mother's grave, I swear it," the corporal said almost angrily.

"And is that coffeepot still here?" Jimmy Piper asked.

The soldier pointed to the chair. "Well, I remember setting the pot down right there, kind of under the chair so I wouldn't knock it over." He pointed at the chair and then took a few steps and bent over to have a look. "Hey, it's not here!" he exclaimed. "Just the cup and saucer."

"The pot must be around here somewhere," McKenzie said, looking at the floor up and down the hallway. "I specifically told those in charge to give strict instructions to the staff not to touch anything on this floor."

"Doesn't surprise me," Jimmy said. "She probably took it with her. I wonder . . ." He went over to the chair and carefully picked up the coffee cup and saucer. The cup still contained a good third of the coffee. Jimmy swirled the remnants around in the cup and then smelled it. "Yes, this should be enough," he muttered, nodding to himself.

"The lady took the coffeepot, but left the dishes?" the corporal asked, a confused look on his face. "That pot was still half full. Why would she do that?"

"I'll let you know later when I'm sure," Jimmy replied. He turned to McKenzie. "My trunk is down in a wagon. I'm going to get Kirkland to set me up in a room somewhere so I can run a few tests. Once I'm set up, I'll return for that coffee cup . . . seems the best place for me to start my portion of the investigation."

"Thanks, Jimmy. Let me know if you need anything," McKenzie said. Then he and Harry again went over with

Jones exactly what happened that night and morning of the kidnapping.

Some fifteen minutes later, two bellhops came huffing and puffing up the stairs, balancing a heavy steamer trunk between them as Jimmy called out instructions and warnings to them in an increasingly frantic voice.

"Lift up the back end! You're shifting the weight too much to the left! Careful, there are beakers . . . glass . . . in there! Do you have any idea how fragile many of the instruments . . .?"

McKenzie could see that the two young men were sweating profusely under their uniforms, ready to collapse, so he stepped forward. "Put the trunk down, boys. Thank you."

The two bellhops stood, red as apples from the exertion they had expended. McKenzie tried to get Jimmy calmed down while the two young men caught their breath.

"I swear nobody has any respect for the property of . . ." Jimmy was saying, but the chief detective interrupted him to make room for two more bellhops arriving at the top of the stairs with a long table for Jimmy's use. Apparently Kirkland was attempting to keep their activities out of the eyes of the other guests by putting Jimmy in a room down the hall, keeping all this activity on the fifth floor. The two men carried the table to the room. After a bit of a racket could be heard, the two bellhops came and helped the other two move the trunk in the room while Jimmy followed along on their heels, once again pointing out the fragility of his possessions.

When the four young men came out of the room, Harry walked over and slipped a generous handful of coins into the hands of the fellow farthest back, telling him to split it among the four for their trouble.

As the bellhop offered his thanks and turned to follow the other three, Harry picked his pocket of the coins.

The commotion having died down now, McKenzie turned once again to Alvin Jones, who had remained in the hallway. "Corporal Jones, before we actually enter the room, I'd like you to just stand inside the doorway, look inside, and tell me if you think anything has changed . . . But don't go in just yet."

The soldier complied with the request, and after a minute or so, he nodded. "Yep. Looks to me like everything is just like I found it that morning."

"And you are sure the windows were all locked from the inside?" Harry asked one more time.

"That's correct," Jones replied, seeming not to be bothered by having to answer the same question numerous times. "Doors too. The only door that wasn't locked was the one that connected the lad's room to Mr. and Mrs. Holt's room. I checked several times."

"Thank you, Corporal," McKenzie said. "That will be all for the time being. We appreciate your help. In the meantime, you can return to your unit. Should I have any questions, I will get in touch with you at Benton."

"Mr. McKenzie, would you mind if I just hung around here in the hallway? I liked that kid, and I'd like to help in anyway I can," the soldier said. "Maybe I'll remember something."

McKenzie figured it wouldn't hurt to have Jones there for a while since it would give him a chance to study his behavior a bit more, as well as ask questions of him if any arose. He nodded his head. "Fine, but please don't touch anything . . . unless you're specifically instructed to do so. You never know what could turn out to be a clue," McKenzie explained.

"Yes, sir," Corporal Jones replied, nodding gratefully.

Harry Howser and John McKenzie entered the hotel room and stood at its center.

"All right, Harry, do your thing. Work your magic," McKenzie said with a small smile. "What do you see?"

Howser turned around in a full circle and began stomping around the room like a man squashing bugs with his feet.

"What in the world are you doing, Harry?" McKenzie asked, annoyed at the noise.

Howser grinned. "If I were doing a vanishing act and this was a stage, I'd have a trapdoor all set and ready to disappear through," Harry told his boss as he pulled aside the rugs. He shifted the missing boy's bed and then checked the floor underneath it.

"Got it now," McKenzie said. "You're trying to find a hollow sound under the floorboards."

Harry nodded. "Right, but unfortunately there aren't any. John, get the corporal to lend me his sword, would you?"

McKenzie had learned long ago not to be surprised at anything Harry Howser said or did.

Remaining at the doorway, the corporal drew his sword from its scabbard and handed it over very carefully. Harry took it and began lightly poking it into the coffered ceiling.

"What's he doing now?" the soldier asked McKenzie, puzzled.

McKenzie shrugged and shook his head. "Don't have a clue."

"A trapdoor could easily be hidden in this coffered ceiling," Harry explained. "And with a trapdoor, you could use pulleys, ropes, or wires to raise or lower something . . . or someone. A young boy doesn't weigh that much." He continued talking and stabbing lightly around the edges of the wood beams where they were joined. "Nope, nothing hidden up there. That ceiling's solid," Harry announced, standing there with a frown on his face, looking up at the ceiling as if he had missed something.

"What if they opened the door with a master key while I was asleep, pulled the kid out, and then used the same key to lock the door when they left?" Corporal Jones asked.

McKenzie thought a moment. "It's possible, I suppose, but

I doubt it. The chair is positioned close to both hallway doors. Someone standing there, fiddling with a lock, so close to your chair would have risked awakening you. I don't think they would have done that." McKenzie shook his head in frustration. "No, I think that would be too big a gamble, even for someone as bold as these people are."

"You really think so, John?" Harry asked.

"Well, it seems to me any noise, even a small one, that close to an armed guard . . . even one who's asleep . . . might wake him. But it's something to keep in mind to consider once we know more."

The two men had been searching the room for almost forty-five minutes when Jimmy yelled out from down the hallway.

"I've got it! I was right!"

"We're coming, Jimmy," McKenzie called as he and Harry headed for Jimmy's makeshift workroom. Corporal Jones lagged behind, but he was as curious as McKenzie and Harry were.

"I've got it," Jimmy announced with a large grin on his face. "Trichloroacetaldehyde monohydrate, two, two, two-trichloro-one, one-ethanediol!" the young scientist said. He held up a glass beaker with something in it.

"English please, Professor," Harry said, shaking his head impatiently.

"Chloral hydrate," Jimmy replied. "I found traces of it in the corporal's coffee cup."

"Chloral hydrate?" Corporal Jones asked, impressed that someone who appeared so young could spout out such scientific sounding words and know what he's talking about. "What's that?" he asked.

"Ever heard of knockout drops, Corporal?" Jimmy replied.

The soldier nodded. "Yeah. I've been around enough bars to have heard of 'em."

"Well, you are looking at the remains of what was in your coffee and the chloral hydrate," Jimmy said with a smile, feeling quite proud of himself.

"Knockout drops? Really?" the soldier asked, surprised.

"Relax, Corporal. This just means that sergeant of yours won't be getting his pound of flesh from you, since it appears you were intentionally drugged as part of the whole scheme," McKenzie said confidently. "All this information will be passed on to those who need to hear it." He paused. "How they knew the Holts were staying here and that there would be a guard stationed at their door is very troubling."

A visibly evident look of relief washed across Corporal Jones's face. "So that cleaning lady must have been in on it. Why that evil bi—witch!"

"I'd say so," McKenzie said, with a slight smile. "Furthermore, this hotel has no record of a maid fitting the description you gave us working the . . . what was it she called it . . . ah, yes, the graveyard shift."

"Well, I'll be dam—darned," Corporal Jones said, shaking his head in disbelief.

"We all may be, if we don't get that boy back," McKenzie said as seriously as he could, since he wanted to smile at the fact the young man kept stopping himself from swearing, as if he was around his parents or a preacher.

"So unless the kid is invisible, we can now assume the cleaning lady . . . whoever she was . . . helped get him out of the hotel somehow," Jimmy posited. "It seems to me it's obvious she took the coffeepot away so no one else would drink from it and find out it had been spiked."

"Wouldn't going back for the pot be just as risky as fiddling with the lock?" Corporal Jones asked.

"Who said she came back for the coffee? We don't know

when the pot was taken," Jimmy said in a somewhat dismissive tone.

McKenzie stepped in before this turned into a speculative debate taking up far too much time. "We don't know when she took the coffeepot," he began, "but we also don't know if she was alone or not once the corporal got knocked out. As for the lock . . . maybe it's as simple as she didn't know how to pick a lock. We're still at the beginning of this investigation, gathering information that will help find the boy. Let's learn as much as we can as fast as we can and leave the speculation for another time."

"But there is one other thing, John," Harry said, thinking out loud. "Why take the risk of relocking the door you just picked? It just doesn't make any sense to me."

"No, it doesn't," McKenzie agreed, mulling over the fact that what Harry said was true. "So maybe they didn't use this door after all."

"I can't figure that one out yet," Harry said, "but my guess is that once the boy was taken out of his room, he was hidden in that laundry cart. The one the corporal mentioned. That was done either by this Clara, or by others working with her."

"He could have been hidden underneath the linens . . . that would have made it easy to push the cart right out of here," Jimmy opined.

"But it still doesn't explain how they got Andy out of that room," McKenzie reminded them, glancing back into the room. "No trapdoors in the ceiling or floors . . . you said so yourself, Harry." The chief detective kept thinking about the room, then he said: "Harry, you and Jimmy go back into the room . . . I need an answer as to how they got Andy out. And we don't have one. I want one before we leave here."

"What about the Holts' bedroom?" Jimmy asked. "Shouldn't we be checking that?"

“They knew the room the boy was in,” McKenzie theorized. “Besides, they wouldn’t have risked waking the parents when it was Andy they wanted.” Turning back to the soldier, he added: “Corporal, like I said, you have nothing to be ashamed about now that we’ve learned that something had been put in the coffee.”

“Except for being too gullible, I guess,” the soldier said sheepishly.

The detective shook his head. “Alvin, I’ve been doing this for a long time now, and I think I’ve become a fair judge of men. I think it’s safe to say that had they sent some pretty, young redhead to cozy up to you, you probably would have suspected something and immediately reacted. While the other hand, who would ever suspect a matronly hotel housekeeper just doing her job?”

“Thank you for that, sir,” Jones said, grateful for the detective’s vote of confidence and trust.

“Someday, you and this old marine will get together and have a drink or two while I tell you stories about how I’ve been fooled by women over the years,” McKenzie said, and they both laughed.

“Hey, boss, I think we might have something here!” Jimmy Piper called out.

McKenzie went in the room with Jones close behind. “Stand here, and remember, don’t touch anything, Corporal.”

Jimmy Piper was on the floor, crawling around the room on his hands and knees, occasionally studying something he found through an oversize magnifying glass.

“What is it, Jimmy?” McKenzie asked, his curiosity piqued.

“I found some scratch marks on the floor by to this big armoire,” Jimmy informed him. “They don’t seem to match up with anything else in the room, as far as I can tell.”

"Here, Professor, let me have a look at it with that glass of yours," Harry said, reaching for the tool. He took his time, looking at the pattern of marks on the floor, measuring their width, and spent a minute or so studying the room and the large furniture chest before letting out a triumphant shout. "Got it! Great work you did there, Jimmy," the magician said, thumping the scientist on the back.

"Figured it out did you, Harry?" Jimmy asked sarcastically.

"You bet I did, kid. See how these scratches go sideways parallel to the wall?" Harry asked, indicating the barely visible marks with his finger.

"Yeah, I see that," the young professor replied, but he still wasn't sure what the magician was pointing out. "So?"

"John, give me a hand here," Harry ordered. "Now watch this, Professor."

Harry put a shoulder to the side of the armoire and, with McKenzie's help, slid the cabinet sideways to reveal a large opening in the wall.

"*Voila*!" Harry announced with a sweep of his arm at the wall. "I give you the elusive trapdoor . . . though it's not an actual trapdoor."

"A passage leading into the next room over," McKenzie mumbled to himself, relieved at perhaps discovering the method by which this crime had been committed.

Harry crawled in through the hole with its precisely cut edges and disappeared into the darkness.

"There's a space between this room and the next," he let them know. "It feels like an alley." Harry's hand shot back into the room. "Hand me your matches, John."

McKenzie obliged and waited impatiently, catching a whiff of sulfur. "What do you see, Harry?"

Then: "There's a dumbwaiter at the far end."

"That's how they got the boy out!" McKenzie shouted as if Harry had discovered gold.

Jimmy stood there transfixed; then, he began to hypothesize: "They sent somebody up in the dumbwaiter . . . that person pushed the armoire over. Then they took Andy out through the hole in the wall. Clara kept watch . . ."

"But how did they know about the dumbwaiter?" McKenzie asked. "It can't be common knowledge."

"That's got me stumped too," said Jimmy.

"As soundly as most kids sleep, I'll bet the boy didn't even wake up when they moved the armoire," Harry said as he entered the room again, not having heard McKenzie's question. "Or maybe they gagged him to keep him quiet. But, either way, all the kidnappers had to do once they pulled the boy through the opening was reach through and slide that big cabinet back into place. Somebody went to the trouble of attaching a couple of handles to help move it back," he explained, pausing before continuing. "Then, I bet they put the kid in the dumbwaiter and sent it down to . . . wherever it goes . . . the kitchen? And no one the wiser. Especially not at that hour, when there probably aren't many people around. Pretty slick, I'd say."

McKenzie thought about it for a moment. "So now we're sure there were at least two involved." He turned to the soldier. "Corporal Jones, your work here is done. Thank you for the help. You can return to your outfit. The rest will be up to us now."

The soldier snapped to attention and saluted. "Thank you, sir," he told McKenzie. "I feel indebted to you men for all the work you do and for helping clear me, so if you need me for anything, I'd be honored to help. Now, with your permission . . ."

McKenzie returned the salute. "Granted."

Corporal Jones shook the hands of Jimmy and Harry before leaving.

McKenzie and Jimmy both explored the secret passage with the help of one of the oil lights.

"Maybe we should check the hotel's register to see who stayed in these rooms . . . or even the rooms on this floor . . . in the past couple of months," Jimmy suggested.

McKenzie shook his head. "I'm almost certain they would have used fake names and addresses. No sense wasting our time." The detective thought a moment and grinned. "But, on second thought, that does sound like something we could pass on to our Secret Service friends. They could compare the handwriting on the ransom letter with the signatures in the guest book. I want you to go see them, Jimmy" he said. "Find out what progress they'd made on the paper. I also need you to follow up on local sources of chloral hydrate."

"On it, boss," Jimmy replied eagerly.

"John, maybe I could use my sources in the theater to see if there are any actresses who fit the description of that cleaning lady," Harry Howser suggested.

McKenzie considered his request. "So you think she might be an actress?"

"Well, if she isn't a professional, she certainly should be. She was calm under pressure, playing the part perfectly without raising Jones's suspicion. Yeah, it's definitely a possibility. Might take us nowhere, but there's no harm in checking it out."

"Yeah, Harry, it's a good idea," McKenzie agreed. "Maybe look for an actress with financial difficulties or criminal behavior in her past?"

"Well, that would cover all of them. They're always hard up for money which can lead to thievery . . . so there you have it," Harry said. "Like I said, John, it may be a long shot, but I'll see what I can dig up."

"That's all I ask, Harry," McKenzie said. "And before you

go, have Kirkland line up staff interviews for tomorrow as well. Somebody may know something about this Clara. And, more importantly, find out what he knows about that hidden passage. So, if that's it for now, we'll all meet back at my suite, eight in the morning. By that time, Alicia should have arrived in town."

Harry nodded. "It'll be good to see her again."

"Why is that?" McKenzie asked, trying to make it sound more like a joke in order to hide his growing nervousness about her arrival. McKenzie, who was generally comfortable around women, found himself at a loss as to how to behave around her.

"Yeah, it will be good to see Ali, John," Harry said in an exasperated tone, having picked up on the irritation in McKenzie's voice and attempting to break him down a little, get him to admit he was smitten, now that the others had left the room. Harry liked and respected McKenzie, but he felt the man played things too close to the vest, never volunteering any information about himself.

"I suppose that's it for the day, then, Harry," McKenzie said. "See you at eight tomorrow."

Harry left without a word.

CHAPTER SEVEN

Always wary of animals, Harry Howser went to the livery where he asked the hostler to pick out his most docile horse. He had to travel two miles outside the city, which for Harry would be a harrowing trip. He arrived at a sprawling mansion, intact but covered in sweat. The house had been used as a hospital during the war, but now provided shelter for family-less and penniless performers. Its inhabitants were those who had bonded with their own kind once they were too old or infirm to work.

Harry figured it was a long shot that the housekeeper would turn out to be a professional actress, but it was necessary to follow all threads in the investigation. After all, this "Clara" had been able to convincingly and comfortably pass herself off as hotel staff.

As he wandered about, Harry ran into several old friends, but none of them could place the actress with the prominent mole on her cheek. The last person he spoke with was an old acquaintance, a white-whiskered old gent who went by the name of Abe Hamilton.

At seventy-five years of age, Abe had spent a lifetime in the theater and had only recently retired due to a bad case of arthritis, which had forced him into taking things easier. Even at his advanced age, while his body might be failing, Abe's mind was still sharp as a tack. In fact, he was a veritable walking encyclopedia of knowledge relating to show-business performers.

"I've got a lucrative opportunity for a woman in a comedy skit involving a magician with a lady assistant," Harry began. "Now the assistant constantly messes things up for him . . . a variation on plenty of other acts, I know . . . but this will be a comedy with interludes of magic instead of just the usual bawdy jokes."

"Yeah, I can see how that might work as a novelty bit," Abe replied, nodding his head. "So, what's the problem . . . what do you need from me?"

"I'm looking for a particular actress. She was described as being perfect for the part. She's supposed to live around these parts, and I thought you might know her."

"What's her name?" Abe asked.

"That's just it. Some friends told me about her, but they couldn't seem to remember her name."

"Well, you got anything to go on? You know what she looks like?" Abe asked.

Harry described her, reciting everything Corporal Jones had told them, ending with the mole on her cheek by her lips. "I don't remember if it's on her left or right cheek."

"I know all about the forgetting problem . . ." Abe said, then added: "Sounds like Edith Edwards. Right age, right build, has a small but noticeable mole, here." He pointed to the left side of his lips. "If I recall correctly, in her younger days, she specialized in backup roles for the more established actresses. Did both dramatic and comedy parts around the South before the start of the war. You know the character, Harry . . . the older sister, the spinster aunt, that sort of thing. She disappeared for a while after her husband was killed fighting for the Confederacy . . . Yellow Tavern, I believe it was." Abe sat back as if he was thinking hard, before he continued. "Your description sounds like her. She'd be a little older now, more matronly. Heard she was leaving town, on her way to Denver."

"Anything else you can remember?" Harry asked.

The old man thought for a moment. "Just Denver. That's it, and that must have been a couple of weeks back."

"Abe, you've been a big help," Harry said as he stood to go. "By the way, I was wondering if she came from around here. She might still have some kinfolk I could try contacting."

"Don't hold me to it, Harry, but I believe somewhere south of here on the Missouri side of the river."

"Thanks again, Abe. I appreciate your help," Harry said.

"You know, it doesn't take a great actor to recognize a bad one," Abe said, grinning.

Harry didn't move. "How's that?" he asked.

The older man rubbed his whiskers and grunted: "Any decent actress in makeup can play that part you're looking to fill, yet you come here looking for this minor actress. Something is up, Howser. I can smell a carny pulling a con a mile away."

Harry held up his hand. "As God is my witness, Abe, it's all on the up and up. I swear to you there is absolutely nothing here for you to concern yourself about."

"But there's no real job offer, is there?" the old actor asked. It was more of a statement actually.

"There is for me, but I can't tell you any more than that," Harry replied. "Would a donation of . . . say, twenty dollars to the home ease your concern and curiosity?" Harry asked.

Abe shook his head. "Nope. But thirty would. It'd help keep my mouth shut and at the same time feed quite a few hungry actors. You might even learn that she lives with her in-laws here in the city." He wrote the address down on a small piece of paper and slipped it to Howser.

Harry smiled and withdrew his wallet. "All for a good cause, my friend, I assure you."

"Nice to see you, Howser," Abe said sincerely.

"You too, Abe, but remember, we never had this conversation."

"Don't have the slightest idea what you're talking about, son," Abe said, shaking his head. "See, I'm too old now to remember such things clearly." The actor thought a moment and added: "You know, Harry, they say the advantage to getting old and losing your memory is you get to enjoy the same jokes over and over again."

Harry Howser laughed out loud and then left, dreading the ride back to the city.

* * * * *

McKenzie's team had assembled in his suite at eight. Alicia Faye had arrived the night before and had checked in with McKenzie, who was taken by surprise when she gave him a hug when he opened the door to his suite. He hoped he hadn't flinched but the smile drained away from Alicia's lips when she pulled back to look at him. For the next half hour, he filled her in on the case, then Alicia begged off, claiming she was tired from traveling.

But that morning, Alicia's arrival at the meeting was met with enthusiasm, hugs, and laughter.

McKenzie gave the team ten minutes to catch up, then he got right down to business. He brought everyone up to date on their findings of yesterday, focusing on the discovery of the secret passageway.

"Jimmy, what did you find out?" McKenzie asked when he had finished.

Jimmy cleared his throat as if addressing a class of students. "Well, after we finished at the hotel, I went over to the offices of that new department, the Secret Service, because Kirkland, the hotel manager, couldn't meet with me for a couple of hours. Boy, 'secret' is the right word for that group. It took me longer to get inside the door and prove who I was than it did to present my doctoral thesis."

"Just the salient points," McKenzie said to him in his Marine Corps' command voice.

"Um, right," Jimmy muttered. "Those fellows have a rather incredible operation going on. They've accumulated a lot of experts on anything and everything related to printing, counterfeiting, and the methods and equipment that go with it. Very impressive, I must say."

"Jimmy," McKenzie said in a drawn out way.

"So they studied the paper of both the ransom letter and envelope and concluded that it came from a paper manufacturer doing business right here in St. Louis."

"Good. How about Kirkland? Did you get back to him?"

"I did. It seems the passageway was created before the war to be used as a temporary hiding place for runaway slaves. Originally, it was a storage room with an entrance in the hallway, which explains the presence of the dumbwaiter. It was a woman who sheltered the slaves. But Kirkland doesn't know her name or anything about her."

"If he did, would he admit it?" Nelson commented to no one in particular.

Jimmy shot Nelson an annoyed look. "So, as I was explaining . . . Kirkland says it hasn't been used in years and that he had forgotten all about it. And I agree with you, John, that the biggest mystery is how our kidnappers even knew about the existence of the secret room, hall . . . whatever we're calling it."

McKenzie nodded and then looked over at Harry.

"I did some searching into the housekeeper," Harry stated. "Talked with an old actor who knew plenty of people in the business. Based on what he said, it appears that mysterious disappearing Clara may be one Edith Edwards. She is, in fact, an actress . . . a bit player, really . . . whose husband died fighting for the Confederacy. Now guess where she grew up?"

"St. Louis," Alicia said.

"Smart as well as incredibly beautiful," Harry said, flashing a smile in Alicia's direction. "You are amazing, Ali."

"Knock it off, you two!" McKenzie snapped. By now he should have been used to the banter that went on between Harry and Alicia. But it irked him, even though he knew they had been friends for a long time. In fact, just about everything he knew about Alicia had come from Harry.

Alicia idolized her father, who she referred to as Pappy, and had grown up sharing his passionate abolitionist viewpoint. Alicia's mother, on the contrary, had no fervent political viewpoint. She preferred simply to support her husband as best she could, something she assumed any loving wife would do. However, even after years of living all over the country, moving with her family from army base to army base, Alicia's mother never lost her charming but rather thick accent, or her Southern mannerisms.

From living so many different places, Alicia, not surprisingly, grew up with an uncanny ability to mimic people's voices and accents from all over the country. It was a skill Allan Pinkerton had picked up on almost immediately upon meeting her. The fact that she was also strikingly beautiful and an actress who could sing and dance with the best of them, was just icing on the cake, as far as he was concerned.

By the time the Civil War broke out, Alicia Faye, the Queen of the South, was already well entrenched in place as a spy for Union Army Intelligence and the Allan Pinkerton Detective Agency.

When she saw Harry Howser audition for a variety show in Memphis, Tennessee, Alicia realized at once how someone with his skills could be of service in gathering information, as well as passing on or stealing secret messages, documents, drawings, or the occasional photograph. She immediately went to work on the theater manager to help get Harry a job.

"Anything else?" McKenzie said, realizing the entire team had been staring at him while he had been daydreaming.

"Yeah, I have the address of her in-laws. She lives with them," Harry said, proud as a new rooster in a hen house.

"Well, I've got something else," Jimmy butted in as though he were in competition with Harry. "On my own authority, I went and asked our local agents here to investigate apothecaries and manufacturers of certain drugs. They didn't have to since, a while back, a box of chemicals was stolen from a warehouse in the industrial area north of the city. Anyone want to venture a guess on what chemicals went missing?"

"That chloral stuff," Alicia said with a sigh, having learned the facts of the case from McKenzie the night before. Then, before anyone could react, she shouted out: "Hydrate! That's it!"

Lips pursed trying to keep back a smile, but McKenzie looked peeved. "All right, everyone, let's stop with the guessing games for now. Ali's right, you're referring to the chloral hydrate?"

"Exactly," Jimmy said. "That box contained enough of the stuff to put a whole platoon to sleep."

"So it does seems as though our kidnappers might be based right here in St. Louis," McKenzie mused aloud.

"Still, it's a big city with a lot of places to hide, and easy to do if you're from here," Nelson commented, shaking his head.

"Boss, I was just thinking," Harry said. "What if we're wrong and the description we're looking at isn't accurate at all? We have a description of a middle-aged actress with a small mole on her cheek."

"Right . . . so?" McKenzie asked.

"Well, admittedly it's a good lead, but still . . . it might be a dead end. After all, any actress, good, bad, or indifferent, can stick on a fake mole or change her hair color."

"They damned well better be able to," Alicia stated.

"So what are you suggesting, Harry?" McKenzie asked, looking a little anxious.

"I think you need to get Corporal Alvin Jones back over here once we have this Edith Edwards. He can confirm whether she's 'Clara' or not. If he recognizes her, we won't be wasting our time."

"I already took care of that last night. He should be arriving anytime now," McKenzie said just as there was a knock at the door.

Nelson answered it and told McKenzie it was somebody for him.

McKenzie wasn't gone for more than a minute. He walked back into the room, an envelope in his hand. "I just received this from a Secret Service messenger." He opened the envelope and pulled out its contents.

CHAPTER EIGHT

McKenzie smiled as he held up a photograph of a young boy, holding a newspaper chest-high.

He handed it to Jimmy, saying: "The boy in the picture has been positively identified as Andy Holt, the kidnapped child we are looking for."

Jimmy crossed the room to retrieve his magnifying glass. He closely examined the newspaper in the photograph.

"It's the *Daily Missouri Republican*, St. Louis, Missouri. And its date is from two days ago. The boy's hand almost covered it up, but you can still see it."

"Good news . . . finally," McKenzie said.

The team took a moment to celebrate the information that Andy was alive and was here in St. Louis.

"I've been thinking that we may be approaching this too narrowly," McKenzie said when the room had calmed down, "and that we shouldn't rule out professional gangs. It might not be about politics or a grudge. As elaborate as this kidnapping was, it may be a well-organized money grab. So, Alicia, I want you to team up with Pat to visit the bars where the criminal element is known to congregate. You'll be rubbing elbows with all types, so be careful." He paused to study her. "I don't think you should be recognizable as the Queen of the South . . . so you'll need to disguise yourself before you go out."

"He's saying you're looking too classy, Ali," Harry said. "But she's right for the job, John, since she can make a man open up pretty damned easily if she sets her mind to it."

"I'm right here, Harry," Alicia stated loudly. "But thank you for the compliment."

"What about Edith Edwards? We talked about her last night and again today?" McKenzie asked. "Do you recall ever encountering her in any of the troupes you've worked with, Alicia?"

"I honestly don't remember ever meeting any actress who went by that name, or this mole we keep talking about," Alicia said. "Still, if she is an actress and a Southerner, she and I may have crossed paths at some point."

"Just because you don't remember her doesn't mean she hasn't seen you," McKenzie said. "So, because we don't know anything about her, what she does, and where she goes . . . we have to be cautious. The last thing we need is this woman bumping into you and recognizing you some place where she knows you wouldn't go. That's why I have to insist that you be on your guard at all times."

One of the most refreshing aspects of Alicia's personality was her total lack of ego. She might have been one of the most beautiful women ever to grace the stage, but behind the scenes she was as down-to-earth as any girl you could find. And she could take a joke and dish one out with the best of them.

"Pat, it'll be up to you to watch out for her," McKenzie said. He had wanted to accompany Alicia himself today, since their only conversation had been all business, but he had the interviews with the staff at the hotel to conduct.

There was a knock at the suite door. Pat answered it and ushered Corporal Alvin Jones into the room.

"Excellent!" McKenzie gushed as the young man walked over and stood at attention close to the group. He was introduced to Alicia, and then McKenzie got right down to brass tacks, having pulled a few strings to have the corporal work with the team for as long as needed.

"Glad you made it, Jones. We brought you in for one purpose . . . to identify the housekeeper. No contact with her is necessary. And remember, we're not charging up a hill here, bayonets fixed and at the ready, Corporal," Captain McKenzie said.

"Understood, sir," the soldier replied. In spite of being cleared of any wrongdoing while guarding the Holts, it was obvious that he still felt personally obligated to right the wrong that had occurred.

"All right then," McKenzie said. "Excellent. You'll be working with Harry at least for the day."

McKenzie looked the soldier square in the face. "I'll tell you what, Corporal. If and when the time comes for a confrontation, I'll assign you to Sergeant Nelson so the two of you can cover our arses. Trust me on this one, there's no finer man to side with in a fight than Nelson."

Corporal Jones smiled. "Yes, sir, you've got a deal."

McKenzie turned to Harry. "You track down Edith Edwards's in-laws' home. When you find it, try talking to someone there . . . I'm sure you can spin some yarn about why you're looking for her. Finding her is paramount to our investigation. And if, for some reason, the family won't cooperate, keep watch on their house in case she shows up. Then it's up to you, Corporal Jones, to get a good look at her.

"We'll find her, John," Harry assured him.

McKenzie looked over at Jones, and back at Harry. "Get him

into civvies and a big hat, Harry, something that will shadow his face."

"How about me?" Jimmy asked anxiously. "What am I going to be doing, John?"

"Professor, you're going to go to the warehouse from where the chloral hydrate was stolen," McKenzie said. "See what you can learn about the theft. If they give you any trouble, remember to flash your Pinkerton badge, but don't use the senator's letter of authority there under any circumstances. Tell them the Pinks are investigating a series of robberies like theirs . . . nothing about the kidnapping though. See if you can determine whether or not it could have been an inside job. Anyone could be in on the abduction . . . owners or workers. Everyone is suspect," he said. "And I want you all to remember when you're asking questions that half this state was Southern in its sympathy, and that Senator Schurz was a Union general. Gettysburg led to the South's downfall, and it was Carl Schurz who led troops for the Union army against Lee's army there. We still have to keep that in mind as long as we don't know the motive behind the kidnapping."

"Understood," Jimmy said, looking very sober. "But won't the owners be suspicious of me, anyway? After all, they were the ones robbed. If an investigation is going on, wouldn't they be aware of it?"

"Yes, and that's why you say it's a series of thefts involving chemicals," McKenzie said.

"That sounds plausible," Jimmy agreed.

"If they're willing, get a look at their record," McKenzie went on. "I know you're as talented with numbers as you are with scientific methods, etcetera. And make sure you watch how they react to your questions. Do they seem nervous . . . agitated . . . those kinds of things. Find out any unusual resignations or firings, even unexplained absences. And who has access to the chemicals on a daily basis. These are the things that might be helpful."

Jimmy Piper nodded as he filed the questions away in his head.

"Then," McKenzie continued, knowing Jimmy had more energy that the rest of the team combined, "if you have time, get over to the paper manufacturer. You should find it on the Secret Service report. See if you can get a list of the stores in the area that might have bought a supply of said paper and run them down."

"I understand, John," Jimmy said. "That's plenty to do, and it may take a while."

As an ex-Marine Corps captain, McKenzie was rather old school, and he always found it disconcerting that someone as young as Jimmy would address him by his first name. On the other hand, he did realize that when it came to smarts, the young professor was probably a lot smarter than he was or would ever be.

"I need not remind you that time is of the essence here," McKenzie said. "We're more than halfway to the deadline."

"What are you going to be doing today, Captain?" Patrick Nelson asked. He was always concerned about his ex-commander's welfare and sometimes acted more like a mother than a frontline fighter.

McKenzie smiled as he told them: "As I am sure you all know, as a former military officer, I am therefore a gentleman, ordained by the Marine Corps and authorized by an act of the government of the United States of America. So, given my high status and remarkable social graces, I will be hobnobbing with the elite of St. Louis society in several of their fanciest clubs. But that doesn't happen till I talk with the staff at the hotel."

"That ought to cost Allan a pretty penny," Harry joked, referring to the head of the agency.

"I'll bet you're right, Harry, but don't worry about it." McKenzie laughed.

"You're probably right, but why are you going all high society on us?" Pat asked.

"Just because these are child abductors, we can't assume that everyone involved is a degenerate lowlife," McKenzie reminded him. "Assume nothing, remember? That's the way we work. Sometimes the biggest criminals . . . I mean the ones running things . . . are often those who travel in the finest company and are seen as people with the highest standards."

"You got that right," Sergeant Nelson agreed.

"Also, I meant to tell you that Allan has agents working other angles, infiltrating pro-South groups with a grudge against the North and our government. They're to report their findings to me."

"Yeah, but there's always that lone wolf type, who can slip through the cracks," Harry pointed out, then added without thinking: "As we all know."

"Let me remind you," McKenzie said, "that even John Wilkes Booth had financial backers and coconspirators to help him. We just didn't learn enough about the ring in time to stop them. We can never let something like that happen again."

"We won't, John," Alicia said.

"From your lips to God's ears, swee—" McKenzie stopped cold. He had almost called her *sweetheart*. He cleared his throat and ended the meeting.

CHAPTER NINE

Looking as though she came from the roughest part of the city, Alicia's disguise even fooled Nelson when she first came up to him outside the hotel. The ill-fitting, drab, and dirty dress she wore allowed her a freedom she hadn't experienced in a while, since everyone she passed averted their eyes and gave her a wide berth.

As she made her way through the saloons and hangouts, Nelson followed at a discrete distance, occasionally crossing the street opposite to observe some down-on-his-luck fellow who seemed to be taking an interest in her. When she entered a saloon, he would wait perhaps twenty seconds before following her in. And once inside, he made sure to find a spot where he could watch without himself being watched, yet close enough to respond quickly should there be any imminent danger. Not that anyone would be watching Nelson dressed as he was and looking no better off than a poor derelict. He was prepared for battle, carrying a .31-caliber Rimfire derringer in his vest pocket, a Mexican dagger, and a small leather bag filled with sand and buckshot, known as a sap or a blackjack, in the inside pocket of his jacket.

The two spent most of the day going from saloon to saloon,

Alicia sometimes claiming to be looking for part-time work and sometimes passing herself off as a drunk trying to find a free drink. Either way, she got a chance to pick up on conversations that were going on. She knew it was a long shot, but she hoped to overhear something that might be useful.

When she asked for work for a third time, she realized how desperate life had become for both men and women in the city, especially for widows with children who hung on to hope by a thread. Those who were lucky enough to have a job worked for a pittance, their existence rattled by fear of destitution and starvation should they lose the work.

At the next place, Alicia decided to switch tactics. After moving around the tables, observing a few card games and listening to monosyllabic conversations, she stopped at one where four men were attempting to look engrossed in playing cards while they spoke in hushed voices.

"Have a little mercy for a thirsty miss?" she asked the men, sidling up between two of the players.

One of the group looked up at her with disgust and replied rudely: "Looks like you stopped being a 'miss' a long time ago."

The other three laughed raucously at the joke.

"Well, I never," she said, feigning offense, even though it was precisely the type of response she'd expected. "But I'm thirsty. So how's about it, gents?" she asked, hoping to get an invitation to sit down, thinking they might ask her just so they could keep making jokes about her.

Three of the four shook their heads, but one of them, the least attractive of the quartet, seemed to have had his interest piqued.

"Sure, honey, I'll buy you a drink, but you'll have to give me something in return."

Alicia knew exactly what the man was suggesting and shook

her head. "I'm just asking for you to make a Christian gesture, not bartering for some disagreeable time like you're thinking."

"Turned down by the ugliest wench in the place," one of the other men said, nudging the fellow. "She said spending time with you, Tom, would be 'disagreeable.' Sounds about right to me."

As before, the others at the table broke out in laughter, which both embarrassed and angered the ugly one they had called Tom.

"Just who the hell you think you are, witch?" Tom shouted at Alicia, even though it was his trio of friends who had become insulting. It was now a matter of pride with him, having been rebuffed by this woman, especially in front of his friends. He sat stewing as his friends started talking among themselves. Several minutes passed, and Alicia was getting ready to move on when Tom pushed the table away, almost upsetting the drinks, stood up, and sprang at Alicia, grabbing her by the arm.

"You and me is going out back for a poke whether you want to or not," he hissed in her ear.

Across the room, it was obvious immediately to Nelson that Alicia had run into some trouble.

"Let me go, you bastard!" she cried out. "I ain't that kinda woman!"

Tom leered at her, spittle collecting in the corner of his mouth as her protestations aroused him further. "Well, if you ain't now, then you soon will be," he said lewdly.

Alicia's heart began to pound, because try as she might, she couldn't break free of the man's strong grip.

A moment later, Tom felt fingers burying themselves deep into his shoulder. He glanced back into the face of Nelson, quickly identifying the man as a fighter, what with his bumpy nose, the scar across his eye, and a slight cauliflower ear.

"The lady wants you to leave her alone," Pat said firmly.

"Bug off," Tom replied angrily. "This ain't your business, mister."

Nelson had his right hand in his coat pocket and his eyes on the other men at the table. However, they seemed content to watch and see how things played out.

"Well, for one thing, I don't like to see no woman mistreated. For another, it is my business since she's my sister," he lied. Nelson reached over with his left hand and pulled the man's hand off Alicia's arm.

"I see you's been at the jug again, sis, but now it's time to head home," Pat said to Alicia in a warning tone. "Ma's been worried sick."

"She only goes if and when I say she goes," Tom insisted, stepping in closer.

Pat quickly removed his right hand from his pocket and smacked the ruffian over the head with his sap, and Tom collapsed like an anchor sinking into water.

"I don't think so," Pat said without a trace of a grin, adding to Alicia: "We're going home now." Then he started to lead Alicia away from the table.

"Hey, tough guy!" one of the men at the table called out, pushing back his chair and trying to stand. "That was our friend you just hit."

"So what?" Pat asked, turning to face them while pushing Alicia back. As he turned he slipped his derringer to her from behind. "Only as a last resort," he whispered.

"So what, he asks," one of the men said, chuckling. "We's gonna hit you back is what." The last two men got up from the table, thinking they looked menacing.

"You boys sure you want to fight over scum like him?" the ex-marine asked, pointing at Tom, who hadn't budged since he dropped to the floor.

"Three to one odds is mighty good, so I guess we just take our chances . . . right, boys?" another of the trio said with a sneer. "Now put 'em up, you son of a bitch."

"Glad to accommodate you gents," Nelson said, raising his hands.

"Prove it by dropping that sap first," one of the men said, pulling a dagger from his belt.

"Only when you three drop your weapons," came Alicia's voice from behind Nelson.

The trio shifted their gaze to find Alicia pointing the derringer at them. For several long seconds, the three stood there, wondering whether she was a genuine threat or not. They decided she was when she cocked the little pistol. Two of the men dropped their knives to the floor.

The third man raised his arms. "I'm unarmed," he said in a hoarse voice.

"Come on, brother" Alicia said to Nelson. "Let's just leave this hellhole. Like you said . . . Ma's a-waiting."

"That's right, little boy, run along with little sis," the tallest of the three men said. "Hide behind her skirt, like a sniveling coward!"

Nelson never backed down from a challenge, let alone an insult to his courage. "Sugar," he said to Alicia, "you run along now. I'll join you shortly." Then he nodded toward the doorway, where the unarmed man from the trio was already headed.

"Either of you ever been to New Orleans?" Pat asked, turning back to face the remaining two men, as Tom lay still on the floor, unaware of the world.

It was easy to tell the two considered it an odd question, especially given the situation they now found themselves in.

"Maybe you boys speak a little French?"

"What the hell has that got to do with anything?" one of the ruffians asked.

"So then I can assume you've never heard of *savate*?" the ex-marine asked. *Savate* being a kickboxing system he had learned from a couple of French sailors when he was stationed in New Orleans just before the war.

"No, we's Virginians, born and bred," one replied proudly.

"Inbred seems more like it to me," Pat said with a sneer.

"Why you son of a . . ." the same fellow started to say, but then he stopped and rushed Nelson instead, attempting to set up a roundhouse punch.

Nelson had his hands held chest-high, but instead of reacting to the rush by punching back, he kicked the man just below his lead knee. The bully went down, yelping in pain.

Sergeant Nelson next gave the remaining man a "come and get it" gesture with his fingers as he rose up on the balls of his feet with his legs slightly apart in a solid but flexible front stance. He knew there was no time for niceties like there would be boxing under Marquess of Queensberry rules. He was ready to attack one of the three most critical areas on the human body, almost guaranteed to incapacitate an opponent: the eyes, the throat, or the knees. But not the groin, since Nelson knew that though a kick there could be effective, it seldom connected, because men learned from an early age to protect that overly sensitive area, which minimized its value as a target of opportunity.

As the last man tried to rush him, Nelson connected by holding his arm straight out, his fingers extended and rigid, and jamming them right into the man's throat as he ran at him. His fingers acted as a blunt spear, and the attacker reached up to his throat as he doubled over, gasping for air. Nelson put a hand on the man's back and used it to support his weight as he side-kicked the man's solar plexus.

It hadn't taken the sergeant much more than a couple of minutes to incapacitate the four men without so much as working up a sweat. He surveyed the room like he was looking for trouble. Almost every man in the room turned his head away.

Pat looked toward the saloon door, where he saw Alicia standing, shaking her head, a Cheshire cat grin on her lips.

"I thought I told you to get out of here, Alicia," he said with annoyance after he walked over.

"Well," she replied softly, "I was worried about you. You could have been hurt, and I have your gun."

"That'll be the day," the sergeant said, looking Alicia straight in the eye. "Come on, let's go," he said, then he took her gently by the arm and led her out the door. He didn't bother to look back.

"You don't think they might be suspects?" Alicia asked.

"Not a chance," Pat replied confidently.

"How can you be so sure?" she asked.

"Aside from their incompetence and their orneriness, if they were involved in a plot as big as this, there is no way they would risk getting into a confrontation that could lead to bringing in the police.

"You're probably right," Alicia said.

"Besides, even if they were involved, they would have been instructed to lay low and to stay as inconspicuous as possible," Pat added.

"I was suspicious," Alicia explained, "because they seemed secretive. They weren't paying any attention to the card game they were playing, and they weren't drinking."

"Probably some ex-soldiers out of work and low on funds trying to bury their troubles in one drink they nurse for hours," Pat opined. "I guess you were right to check them out."

"I really appreciate your help, Pat," Alicia said, "but, like I said before, I could have handled the situation."

They walked for a block in silence. Suddenly, Alicia stopped and smiled up at Pat, saying: "Maybe we should keep this little incident under our hat when it comes to the others, especially . . . Well, you understand."

"Just doing my job," he replied with a smile.

"Just make sure you let me do mine too," Alicia said as she slipped her arm through his as they walked down the uneven cobblestones.

CHAPTER TEN

Harry Howser and Corporal Alvin Jones had the buggy they were riding in stop a block away from the address that Abe Hamilton had given Harry.

"How are your eyes, Jones?" Harry asked.

"Don't need glasses," he said in response.

"That's good to hear," Harry said, handing him a pair of field glasses. "If you see anyone who looks remotely like the housekeeper, coming or going, take a look through these field glasses to make sure. Try not to let anyone see you doing it," Harry warned. "But if someone does see you, say you're a bird watcher."

"What if she gets away?" Jones asked. "Should I follow her?"

Harry shook his head. "Just try to get a good look at her. If you're not sure if it's her, then we wait and try again. So all you have to remember is . . . see but don't be seen while you're seeing."

"Got it," the soldier said with a quizzical look on his face.

"Then you run back here and get me, and we'll trail her at a safe distance. Keep in mind, Alvin, that she's not the one we're after ultimately, Andy is. She's just the one we think can lead us to where the boy is being held," Harry reminded him. "Relax, Corporal, your part is quite simple. See, but don't be seen, and don't attract any undue attention to yourself . . . or me," Harry cautioned.

"Got it," the soldier said, glancing around, although Harry wasn't sure Jones actually got it. "I'll go behind that tree over there," he said, pointing to a large maple near the street corner.

Harry shook his head. "I don't think that's a good idea." He looked up and down the street. "See that bench over there?" Harry asked, pointing. "Looks to be made of rocks."

"Yes, sir," the corporal replied after honing in on the spot Harry had selected.

"Go sit over there. Be patient. I'm going to the house to see what I can find out."

"Yes, sir. I got it, sir. See but don't be seen," Jones repeated.

"And, Corporal," Harry added before they separated.

"Yes, sir?"

"You aren't in uniform now, so loosen up your posture. You need to act more like a damned civilian. One last thing . . . stop calling me 'sir.' I work for a living."

Harry walked down the street toward the modest two-story home believed to be owned by the Edwards. He took a deep breath before proceeding up the steps to the front porch. Compared to many of the others on the street, the Edwards' home was well cared for, with flowers blooming in the garden beds on both sides of the porch.

Before knocking, Harry glanced back over his shoulder to make sure Corporal Jones was out of view, hoping Jones wouldn't be conspicuous in this neighborhood which was very quiet. The last thing he wanted was to have the corporal arrested for being a Peeping Tom or a burglar.

Finally, Harry lifted the large, horse-head door knocker and tapped on the door three times. No one answered, so Harry knocked again. The door finally opened a few inches.

A silver-haired lady had answered it hesitantly. "May I help you?'" she asked, the door remaining mostly closed.

Harry removed his hat and bowed slightly. "Good afternoon, madam, my name is Sawyer. Harry Sawyer. I hope I am not disturbing you, but I understand that a certain actress . . . a Miss Edith Edwards . . . lives here. Am I at the correct residence or am I mistaken?" he asked.

The lady nodded. "Edith is my daughter-in-law. May I ask why you are inquiring about her?" The door edged open about ten inches.

Harry smiled broadly. "Oh, it's nothing to worry about at all, Mrs. Edwards." He held out one of his business cards which he had selected from his stack of business cards, identifying Harry as anything from bank director to tarot card reader. He had learned from experience that people tend not to ask for additional identification once a person introduces himself and then deposits a business card in their hand.

"I am a professional producer and am putting together a show," he began. "A friend recommended your daughter-in-law as a possible actress for the role. It is an entirely professional and respectable dramatic show, I assure you. A touch of humor here and there, I confess, but nothing risqué or untoward. I do have references with whom I can put you in touch . . . if you'd like."

Mrs. Edwards seemed to relax somewhat. "Oh, how nice that would be. Edith just loves the theater, but since the war of Northern aggression ended . . . well, you know, everything has changed."

Harry had to consciously remind himself that as far as Southern sympathizers were concerned, it had not been a Civil War or Rebellion, but rather a legitimate secession from an oppressive federal government.

"Is Miss Edith in for callers?" Harry asked, confident that if she were, Mrs. Edwards would not hesitate to fetch her for him.

"I'm so sorry to tell you she is not," Mrs. Edwards replied graciously.

Harry thought fast. "Well then, I would ask that you pass on my business card. And, with your permission, might I request to return when you think she will be available to speak with me? As I said, I really need to fill the role quickly so we can start rehearsing as soon as possible."

"Well, she's been going out in the morning around nine, and she returns by six in the evening," Mrs. Edwards informed him.

"Oh, so she already has work. Is it a play or show of some sort? Perhaps I could take in the performance and see her work myself."

Mrs. Edwards shook her head. "No, no, I don't believe it has anything to do with acting, though I can't say with any certitude what it is she is doing. All I know is she is required to keep a rigid schedule. You could stop by tomorrow evening perhaps."

"Well then, Mrs. Edwards, I will bid you adieu. It was a delight meeting you. I will try to return tomorrow night around . . . six thirty then . . . to discuss the matter with her, if that meets with your approval."

"I'm sure it will be, Mr. . . ." She glanced down at the business card. "Sawyer, Mr. Sawyer. Generally, we don't dine until around seven thirty, so it shouldn't be an inconvenience at all. Will an hour be sufficient to conduct your business with Edith?" Mrs. Edwards asked, smiling when Harry nodded yes to her question, and then she dismissed him rather hastily by closing the door.

CHAPTER ELEVEN

"Any luck, boss?" Nelson, the first to arrive at their meeting scheduled for late that afternoon, asked from the arm of a chair on which he was perched. He was frustrated because he and Alicia had come up empty in their rounds.

McKenzie didn't answer immediately as he closed the door, shrugging out of his coat. Finally he shook his head. "I spent the afternoon visiting the St. Louis Social Club and the Quoits Club. Aside from sipping some rather fine wine and watching rich gents tossing metal rings about, I came up blank."

"Quoits?" Corporal Jones asked as he scurried into the room, fearing he had missed something.

"Yeah," McKenzie replied, "it's an odd name, isn't it? From what I gather, rich gentlemen with too much time on their hands try to land these rings around a peg . . . think I heard someone call it a hob. Quite boring"

"Sounds exciting," Harry said sarcastically, putting in his two cents' worth, having entered the room as McKenzie explained the game.

"It isn't," McKenzie replied, annoyed by his task in the

investigation. "And I still have the Leisure Club and the Banker's Club left to visit. But maybe something will come to light." He didn't sound too optimistic.

Jimmy Piper looked up from the paperwork he was reading, having quietly come into the room behind Corporal Jones. "I might have something here, boss," he said with a measured excitement.

"Hell, the rest of us are all grasping at straws, so out with it, Jimmy," McKenzie said.

"Well, I came up blank with regards to the employees at the paper mill. Nobody there seemed to have been at the wrong place at the wrong time, and, with respect to the owners, I don't think they could ever be criminals or fanatics. They just want to keep the family business in operation."

"So did you find out anything that might be useful, Jimmy?" Alicia asked impatiently, even though she was the last to arrive, having made a stop on her way to the meeting.

"Well, they let me take these records, and here"—he ruffled through the ledger pages—"I discovered that the mill produced only a limited amount of the paper in question, and practically all of it was sent to one stationary shop here in the city."

"That it?" McKenzie asked.

"No! Based on that, I took it upon myself to check out the shop . . . Beauregard's Fine Paper," Jimmy told them. "The store's been around for decades and didn't seem to be a hotbed of criminal activity either, but the owner . . . a man named Phineas Applethwaite, very well educated . . . told me that he sold the majority of that specific paper to a man named Jason Longwood."

"Did you ask what business this Longwood is in?" Patrick asked, scribbling the name in his notebook.

"Well, I haven't had time to track down any specifics, but

it appears he owns a couple of warehouses and is involved in shipping, Somebody said he owns a second steamboat, but I couldn't verify it. He is a Southern sympathizer."

John McKenzie rubbed his chin, repeating to himself sotto voce: "Jason Longwood. Jason Longwood." After several minutes, he announced: "I think I met the man in that first club I went to today."

"Which one was that?" Alicia asked. "I don't think I was here when . . ."

McKenzie nodded his head, pulled out a notebook, and began paging through it. "Um . . . let's see. Yes, here it is . . . Jason Longwood. So it was at the St. Louis Social Club. I met so many men in such a short period of time, I started writing down names."

He leaned back against the fireplace, filling his pipe, while the others discussed what they had learned. McKenzie had to concentrate to follow what was being said, because he was trying to recall the faces of the men to whom he had been introduced, but to no avail.

After a bit more discussion, McKenzie ended the meeting by summarizing their individual assignments for the remainder of the day, as well as the next day.

"Pat, I want you to head over to the senator's ranch. Talk with anyone who works in the house as well as the ranch hands. See if you can find out if anyone there has a problem with the senator. Also, find out who has visited in the last month or so."

The ex-marine sergeant nodded his head.

"Make sure you find out if anyone has recently been hired or fired," McKenzie added. "We're still trying to figure out if somebody might be carrying a grudge for the senator."

"Ask about women workers and visitors too," Alicia added to McKenzie's train of thought. "Could have been some temporary kitchen help, or . . . who knows? Maybe this Edwards woman was out there."

"Alicia is right, Pat," McKenzie said. "Women too. And remember, don't bother the senator or his family, unless they come to you."

"Yes, sir," Patrick replied.

"Professor," McKenzie said, directing his attention to Jimmy, "you mentioned warehouses and boats owned by Longwood. I'll be needing a full list of all of this man's holdings, partnerships, etcetera. We may end up having to search his businesses, one by one, if anything . . . anything at all . . . connects him to the kidnapping. You're the best we have for this kind of research, so you get the job. Also, see what you can dig up about him personally."

McKenzie stopped to tamp down the tobacco in his pipe before addressing Harry. "What I need for you to do, Harry . . ."

"Already read your mind," the magician said, interrupting his friend. "Alvin and I will take up posts near the Edwards' home again. Maybe the corporal will get a look at her face and be able to identify her when she gets home tonight. If it is our 'Clara,' then tomorrow we'll follow her every move. Could you arrange for a carriage and driver to pick us up in the morning in case we have to follow her? I'm not riding another horse while I'm on this case."

"I'll arrange it," McKenzie confirmed.

"And what about me, John?" Alicia asked. "Back to the seedy dives?"

"I've been thinking about that," McKenzie said, feeling elated that he had come up with an assignment that would allow them to spend some time together, even if it was work. "This Jason Longwood could be our first real lead, besides the housekeeper . . . so, this evening, you will accompany me to the

St. Louis Social Club as if on a date. Do you think you can get hold of an appropriate dress to wear to the club?"

"I'll find something," Alicia said without hesitancy.

"I've got a contact who should be able to get hold of a few baubles for you to add to your ensemble," he advised her. "By the time we meet tonight, I'll have them for you."

"I've never been to that particular club, but I know its reputation is . . . fancy," Alicia said, her voice taking on a nasal quality when saying the word. "As for Longwood, if we find him, I believe I will have more success at getting close to him than you will have, John."

"Point taken," McKenzie commented distractedly, already becoming concerned by the prospect of Alicia being anywhere near this man who he couldn't recall visually. But, depending upon what they could learn tonight, a feigned relationship with Longwood might be the best opportunity to learn something about him.

"All right, that's it, unless there's something else," McKenzie announced, his eyes traveling the room.

"How'd your interviews go at the hotel?" Pat asked.

"Nobody remembers anything or saw anything," McKenzie replied. "But I did learn that the dumbwaiter goes down to the kitchen."

"Just a thought, John," Harry said, "but maybe we should start discussing just how we plan to get the boy away from whoever has him."

"I was wondering about that too," Nelson said.

"Did either of you come up with anything?' McKenzie asked.

"Well, no I didn't," Pat admitted as Harry shook his head. "If this was the same as anything other abduction, I'd suggest we mount a full-on attack," Pat replied. "But we're trying to save a child."

"Oh, perish the thought of that," Alicia said, shaking her head.

"I think we're putting the cart before the horse," McKenzie cautioned. "We haven't a clue as to where Andy is being kept. So let's table this topic for a time. It's back to work. You all know what you need to do. We can meet back at the hotel tonight around nine, if you need to talk. My suite."

Harry groaned. "I was hoping for at least one night's rest."

McKenzie shook his head firmly "You can sleep when the boy is safely back home with his family. Till then no one rests. Agreed?"

Everyone nodded in agreement. In truth, they were too embarrassed not to.

CHAPTER TWELVE

It was nearly five after six, and neither Harry nor Alvin Jones had seen anyone enter or leave the Edwards' house since they arrived around five in a buggy. The driver had been willing to sit and wait, it being his dinnertime, but that had been around five. Harry was about ready to give up, some twenty minutes later, when he saw a woman walking down the street. Corporal Jones saw her too, and even though the light was failing, the soldier could see her face. It was the woman who had called herself Clara.

* * * * *

The bell tower had just struck five thirty when John McKenzie and Alicia Faye arrived at the St. Louis Social Club, decked out in the finest they could put together on short notice. When they entered the club, McKenzie offered to take Alicia's shawl, but she declined, saying she was a bit chilled. She wore a stunning dark-blue evening gown with a low-cut front that was highlighted with tiny silk flowers and a lace border. The necklace and earrings he had borrowed suited her and what she was wearing perfectly.

In her right hand she carried a blue oriental fan decorated with golden dragons. McKenzie knew that the strut supports of that decorative accessory were made from hardened steel, instead of the usual bamboo, and that their tips were sharpened to a fine point. McKenzie had bought it from a fellow marine who had spent some time in the Orient. But it was Sergeant Nelson who had personally trained Alicia in its use, particularly for self-defense. Regardless of how attractive it looked, open or closed, the fan made a wicked weapon. As McKenzie took her arm, his heart began beating as it had back at the hotel when he saw her for the first time in almost ten months.

They made their way through the large entry and toward the main dining room. When they paused at the entrance, more than a few heads turned in their direction. Given that most of the heads in the room belonged to men, McKenzie knew those looks were directed at Alicia. If he were totally honest with himself, John would have to admit that he too felt the same heartthrob whenever he looked at her.

What he didn't realize, however, was that Alicia Faye had been infatuated with him from the first time they met. Because she valued her work above everything, Alicia had kept her feelings to herself, fearing, as did John, that bringing the subject up could possibly jeopardize their working relationship, as well as their friendship.

"Shall we go on in now, my dear?" McKenzie asked, playing his part as the gentleman escort.

Alicia smiled and carefully raised the fan up to cover the lower half of her face, so that all one could see was the light from the chandeliers glimmering in her eyes. McKenzie found her coquetry most alluring, and as she stood there, he allowed himself to look the full length of her.

Alicia noticed and shook her head. "Not quite yet, John.

I want the total effect to sink in," she said quietly, the fan still covering most of her face.

"For whom?" McKenzie asked, smiling.

"Who says it isn't for you," Alicia teased, keeping her eyes focused on the room, for tonight Alicia was determined to enchant the men in the room while studying them and their behavior. Whether working as an actress, detective, or undercover spy, Alicia was well aware of the spell she could cast on men. Tonight she was on the lookout for one type of man, a self-assured, strong-willed, dominant male.

Alicia let McKenzie know it was time to head in with a little tug on his arm. Once they were in the room, Alicia swayed to the music coming from a stage to their left where a band played.

"Would you recognize this Longwood fellow on sight?" Alicia whispered.

"I told you I remember being introduced to someone with that name, but there were others in the group at the time and whoever this Longwood is, he didn't stand out," McKenzie explained. "Let's try to get as many names as we can while we mingle."

A waiter in tails walked past with a silver tray holding glasses of wine. As he passed, McKenzie took a glass for himself and another for Alicia, not so much to drink as to appear as though they fit in with the other merrymakers.

The pair wandered the room, ever alert but smiling as they met people. McKenzie had gained access to the club with fake papers identifying himself as a gentleman plantation owner from Louisiana. He had lost his lands, or so went his cover story, when the Federals took over New Orleans during the war, and he had escaped by boat with a substantial part of the family's wealth intact.

McKenzie was fairly confident he wouldn't be too closely questioned inside the club, but if it were to happen, he was prepared, for he was well acquainted with the geography, the personalities, and the politics of New Orleans, having served there for a year in the military.

"What's behind all those doors men keep disappearing into . . ." Alicia began to ask, but then she shook her head. "Cardrooms," she answered herself. "Might be awkward wandering from room to room, asking for one specific name, John."

"I've only seen one man I met earlier, and I know he's not Longwood. But I have an idea."

"What's that, John?"

"The one thing guaranteed to draw everyone back into the room," he said, smiling at her mischievously.

As if she read his mind, Alicia replied: "How will you pull that off?"

They continued to smile at people as they walked around, making small talk with others who would pause and introduce themselves. McKenzie made a point of introducing Alicia as the Queen of the South whenever she caught the eye of a man.

"Alicia Faye! My God, it is you," a rotund gentleman blurted out upon meeting her. His name was Joshua Norcross. "I've seen you perform onstage before, and I must say it was a most enjoyable evening. Allow me to tell you that you're even more beautiful close-up."

Alicia opened her fan and covered her face as if to hide a blush. "Why, sir, you simply flatter me to death." she said in her most coy manner.

"And your voice," the man continued, "was . . . I mean is . . . oh, dear. Let me start over. When I saw you perform . . . your voice was like that of an angel."

That was just the opening McKenzie had been waiting for.

"Mr. Norcross," McKenzie stated, shifting in a bit closer, "you have a talented group of musicians here tonight. Maybe we could impose on Miss Faye to sing something for us?"

From behind her fan, Alicia gave John a piercing look, feeling he was pushing a little too hard.

"Oh, would you?" the man implored Alicia, emboldened by McKenzie's suggestion. "It would be a crowning moment for our club."

Alicia curtsied. "Oh, very well," she said, "if you gentlemen insist."

"But we do," McKenzie said with an exaggerated bow. He found it hard to contain a slight chuckle when she looked back, her eyes shooting fire at him, as Norcross escorted her to the stage.

Alicia walked over to the stage while Norcross ran, clapping his hands together in an effort to get everyone's attention. Once he announced that the legendary actress, the Queen of the South herself, Alicia Faye, was about to sing for them, the place was buzzing, and everyone crowded closer to the stage.

Alicia smiled at the audience, stepped back to whisper a few words to the band's leader, who nodded his head as she took center stage.

McKenzie knew that if the mere mention of Alicia's name didn't draw all the men back into the room, the sound of her voice surely would. As usual, he was not wrong.

Once Alicia started singing "Weeping, Sad and Lonely," the room instantly became silent. Her soft, warm tones emphasized the painful lyrics of the popular wartime ballad.

Dearest love, do you remember
When we last did meet,
How you told me that you loved me,
Kneeling at my feet?
Oh! How proud you stood before me,
In your suit of gray,
When you vow'd to me and country,

To be true always.
Weeping, sad and lonely,
Hopes and fears, how vain.
When this cruel war is over,
Praying! That we'll meet again.
When the summer breeze is sighing,
Mournfully, along!
Or when autumn leaves are falling,
Sadly breathes the song.
Oft in dreams I see thee lying
On the battle plain,
Lonely, wounded, even dying;
Calling, but in vain.

The doors to the cardrooms that had been tightly shut since their arrival suddenly began shooting open as the cardplayers scurried noisily out to see who was singing. They were shushed by others in the audience.

It didn't take McKenzie long to recognize Jason Longwood once he saw his face again. He tried to get Alicia's attention with a subtle dip of his head in Longwood's direction.

Alicia understood McKenzie's cue and directed her gaze to that side of the room. She studied the faces of the men as she neared the end of the song. She was about to bring her eyes back to the middle of the room when they settled on a tall, handsome man with raven-black hair, dressed impeccably. She knew she was looking at Jason Longwood. Her gaze seemed locked on him, but she made her eyes flit back to the middle of the room for the final line of the song. On the last note, they went back to Longwood, and she attempted to make him feel as though she was singing to him alone. Applause and calls of "Brava" filled the room. She watched as the club's members seemed to sense Longwood's presence and parted like the Red Sea as he headed for the stage. She had no idea why, but Alicia suddenly felt chills run down her spine. She smiled as she thought to herself that this man's looks and style would attract the attention of any woman.

Longwood approached her, smiling in a pleasing but practiced manner.

"I heard you sing some time back in Charleston, Miss Faye," he said in a silky tone, "and I must say your voice has only improved with time."

"Miss Faye was kind enough to accept my request to sing for us, Jason," Joshua Norcross explained, trying to crowd in and get closer to Alicia.

Jason Longwood greeted him politely, but then ignored him. "I for one am glad she did," he said. His eyes never left Alicia until he took out an expensive-looking gold pocket watch from his vest pocket and glanced at it.

Turning to Norcross, he smiled. "Joshua, when you came in the club tonight, didn't I overhear you say your lovely wife was expecting you home early?"

Norcross flushed with embarrassment, and Alicia had to open her fan to hide a smile. As far as others were concerned, Longwood might have gotten his point across unnoticed, but, to someone as traveled as she was, his actions were quite obvious to read.

"Why, yes, Jason, thank you for reminding me." The look Norcross gave Longwood was anything but appreciative. Longwood appeared not to notice, or perhaps he didn't care.

"An honor to have met you, Miss Faye, but sadly I must be leaving now," Norcross said and took his exit, a look of irritation on his face when someone asked him a question which he ignored.

As if he noticed John McKenzie for the first time, Jason Longwood bowed slightly and extended a hand. "I apologize, sir, but I didn't catch your name."

"Don't apologize. I didn't throw it out. John McKenzie at your service," he said. "Late of the New Orleans McKenzies."

"We met earlier today, didn't we?" Longwood asked as he studied John's face.

"We did, though briefly."

"I don't mean to intrude on your evening, but do you mind if I ask if you two are together?" Jason Longwood asked. His manner was polite, but Alicia felt as though he didn't have time to waste if Alicia was spoken for.

Shifting so Longwood couldn't see her face, Alicia winked at McKenzie as if to say: *I've got him.*

McKenzie showed no reaction. Instead, he smiled graciously and said in response to Longwood's question: "Goodness, no, we're not a couple. At least, not in the way you suggest. You see, Alicia is my cousin. She arrived in town earlier today, and since she had no plans, I invited her to accompany me tonight. I'm new to the club . . . of course you would know that . . . and I'm looking to invest what I managed to save from those damned Federal plantation burners. No matter . . . Anyway, I thought St. Louis might be a good place to look for a new opportunity or two before I decide where to settle next. I determined that joining the club . . . how shall I say it . . . would put me in close proximity with those to whom I could be of service and vice versa."

"As good an explanation as any, I suppose," Longwood responded. "Cousins, eh? Mr. . . . McKenzie, was it?" he asked, and John nodded. "Would you mind terribly, sir, if I invited Miss Faye to dine with me aboard my paddleboat tomorrow night? I would certainly repay such a debt by listening to your financial proposals at your earliest convenience. If I can't personally be of assistance, I know plenty of businessmen who might be able to help you."

Alicia was about to feign indifference when Longwood quickly turned to her with a disarming smile. "Please understand, Miss Faye, that there is no barter intended in this whatsoever. The decision as to whom you wish to have dinner with is, of course, up to you. I am merely trying to be polite to another gentleman and fellow club member. Apparently one with the same political sympathies as I. Nonetheless, I shall try to help your cousin regardless of your decision. That said, I would be truly honored and delighted if you would kindly accept my offer."

While flattered by Longwood's attention, Alicia felt a growing anger at John, who seemed a little too happy that this potential suspect was taking an interest in her. She recalled that several times, back when they had first met, she had flirted openly with him. He had remained oblivious to her attention then, but tonight, after she arrived at his hotel room, she had felt his hands shaking as he had helped her put on the necklace. She knew she couldn't come out and ask him directly about his feelings, so she decided she would let him think she actually found Longwood attractive, and then she would see if he became even the least bit jealous. She hated to be as conniving as that, but she wanted to know if he had any interest in her.

"You mentioned something about a boat?" Alicia said to Longwood, touching his arm as she did so. She glanced up at John, but his face gave no clue as to what he was thinking.

"I own the *Southern Belle*," Longwood answered, "a paddle wheel. She's the best on the river, and I would love for you to see her. Having the Queen of the South on the *Southern Belle* would be fitting, don't you think?" Jason added. "And I assure you that unlike some of the . . . shall we say, more imposing types," he added in a clever reference to Joshua Norcross, "I promise not to make you sing for your supper."

Alicia laughed. "Sounds lovely. You wouldn't mind if I accepted Mr. Longwood's kind offer, would you, John?" she said, looking up at John with a challenge in her eyes.

"If he's a member of this club, Alicia, I'm sure he is a trustworthy pillar of the community whose credentials and morals are unquestionable," McKenzie replied, bowing slightly, but giving Longwood a solemn look. At times like this, he wished he could just speak his mind.

Jason Longwood smiled. "Kind of you to say so, sir." He turned to Alicia. "Dinner at eight tomorrow night? I'll send a coach for you, if you wish."

"That would be lovely," she said.

"If Mr. McKenzie will leave the details of your accommodations here in St. Louis with Wilfred on the way out, I will handle the rest. Nice to make your acquaintance, sir," he said, extending a hand out to John.

McKenzie smiled and shook hands, gripping Longwood's hand a little harder than his regular handshake. "Likewise."

Longwood gave McKenzie a side glance, then took Alicia's hand in his own and kissed it. "I am very much looking forward to seeing you again, Miss Faye, but sadly I have to return to a card game in which I am winning. I promised some rather unlucky members that I would return to give them a chance to recoup their money. It seems they don't wish to be forced to explain to their wives why they returned home with so much less money than when they left."

"You devils," Alicia said, laughing and shaking a finger at him.

With a chuckle, Longwood bowed, turned, and headed straight back to one of the private cardrooms.

Alicia knew from experience that most men would have hung around longer, believing their attention would somehow make them more endearing to a woman.

But not this man, Alicia thought, pursing her lips. *He knows better. Always leave them wanting more, something everyone in the theater knew and practiced. This Longwood is both very confident and cunning.*

Having accomplished what they had set out to do, McKenzie and Alicia left the club and took a buggy back to their hotel. During the ride they were able to compare impressions.

"I like him," Alicia commented.

"That much was obvious," John replied, annoyance obvious in his voice.

Alicia couldn't help but giggle. "I meant I like him as a prime suspect. What happened back there was all in the line of duty, John, nothing else." Hesitantly, she put a gloved hand on McKenzie's arm to reassure him.

Although her touch sent sparks up his arm, he would not allow himself to show it.

"You know, Alicia, sometimes I think you are a better actress than I give you credit for."

"Do not ever doubt it for a moment," she replied, turning her head and smiling out the carriage window.

CHAPTER THIRTEEN

"Oh, Pat, good to see you. We were getting worried," McKenzie said as Nelson hurried into the suite, dressed more like a cowboy than a detective.

"Did you learn anything of interest at the Schurz's ranch?" Harry asked of Pat, once he was settled in a chair.

"Not much. And I would have been back sooner, but I got thrown by my horse coming back to town when something or another spooked him, and he took off crow-hopping . . . thought I was going to be left out there on my own.

"You're all right, though?" Alicia asked.

"I didn't fall on my bad leg. So back to the ranch. The head of the house staff said there haven't been any new hires for a couple of months, no parties, and no strange visitors. Maybe they're just not remembering . . . Andy not being there. I had a long talk with the senator's foreman, a fellow named Russell Franklin. I was told by the family I could trust him . . . hired by the previous owners over ten years ago. The senator kept him on." Nelson paused to take a drink of water. "So Franklin mentioned one particular hand who had just never fit in with the other hands, and who hadn't worked there long, a Biff Sanders. Midtwenties, sports a handlebar mustache, which he's pretty proud of. Franklin thought Sanders seemed rather disgruntled with the senator even before he got fired for trying to steal some gear from the barn. Anyway, since this was the only person Franklin found even remotely suspicious, I decided to come back to town and try to find him.

"A few of the hands thought he was living in a boardinghouse here in the city. They told me where it was, generally. I got lucky, because, right off, I spotted him leaving the house, so I followed him. He went to a saloon down the street . . . I have the name here somewhere," he said, pulling out his notebook and flipping through it.

"Not necessary, Pat, just go on from there," McKenzie instructed.

Nelson nodded. "Well, after about forty-five minutes, he finally came out and got onto a wagon that took him across town to the riverside district. I never got a good look at who was driving the rig, but I followed it. I'm fairly certain I wasn't spotted." The detective hesitated, referring to his notes once again.

McKenzie knew Pat had a very good memory for details, but, for some reason, when on the job he didn't trust himself and was always referring to his notes.

"Go on, Pat, skip to the finale, as Alicia and Harry might say," McKenzie said, glancing at the two who smiled at the reference.

"Well, sir, the rig finally stopped at one of the piers on the river where this Sanders fellow got out. I saw him go aboard a large paddleboat that was anchored there," he said, stuffing his notepad in his breast pocket.

"Let me guess," McKenzie chipped in. "The *Southern Belle*?"

"That's right," Nelson said, his surprise visible. "That's the name. How in the world . . .?"

"The name of that steamboat keeps coming up," McKenzie said, glancing over at Harry.

"Owned by Jason Longwood," Jimmy added.

"So there's the common link we've been looking for," McKenzie said, leaning forward and tapping his pipe on his hand . "Still, we have no proof the boy is aboard." The lead detective knew the team had already placed the boy on the boat in their minds. He had to keep the team reined in, or the boy could end up hurt or worse. "Anything else?"

"I have something!" Jimmy called out, and McKenzie responded with a nod. "I spent the day visiting three of the warehouses owned by Longwood," the scientist began. "At least those I've learned about. Seems the man has plans to build an empire."

"And?" Harry asked impatiently.

The boy scientist shook his head. "The warehouses looked like . . . well, warehouses. There wasn't any sign of guards or blocked entries. Two were wide open for business and one was shut down and dark. But anyone could walk in and roam around. I couldn't find a thing that aroused my suspicion. What activity I saw looked normal."

"They would hide him in such a way as to avoid precisely that . . . suspicion, I mean," Alicia remarked.

Jimmy looked a little deflated by her observation, but McKenzie reassured him. "No, Professor, I think you are quite right this time. If it is, Longwood would probably stash the boy somewhere that provided him more control than a wide-open, unguarded warehouse."

"And just how do we check that out without storming the boat as Patrick suggested before?" Harry said.

"Already ahead of you for once, Harry," McKenzie said. "We use one southern belle to check out another."

"How . . . what?" Harry started to ask, then stopped and looked over at Alicia. He turned back to McKenzie and said loud and harshly: "No!"

"I already have a dinner invitation aboard the *Southern Belle* tomorrow night," Alicia announced, a satisfied smile on her face. She tipped her head slowly and regally.

"I don't like it, sir," Pat said, agreeing with Harry. "It's too dangerous to send a wo—"

"Don't you dare finish that sentence, Sergeant," Alicia interrupted, shooting him a glare that would have made Lee surrender a year earlier.

Nelson got the message. "I mean, um . . . that it would be dangerous for a person . . . woman or man . . . to go aboard alone."

"I do not intend to go in sword drawn and guns blazing, Patrick," she said, calming slightly. "This is one of these brains-over-brawn instances I'm sure you must have heard about."

Jimmy couldn't help but laugh, which immediately earned him a dark stare, this time from Nelson. "Sorry, I couldn't help myself," Jimmy said, averting his eyes.

"As much as I hate to admit it, I think this is one of those times when feminine wiles may be more valuable than going in guns blazing, Pat," McKenzie advised him, though he was probably more worried about Alicia than any of the others in the room. "Look, we need to have some knowledge about the layout of the boat," McKenzie continued, "and we need to try to find out where that boy is being kept, if he is there. Under the circumstances, Alicia is best suited for the undertaking, especially since she has a personal invitation from Longwood himself. Besides, who would suspect the Queen of the South being a lady detective?"

"Much less one so attractive," Harry chimed in.

"Touché, Harry," Alicia teased, opening her fan coyly.

"Ohhh, be careful with that, honey," Harry said, knowing the secrets of the fan.

"I'm almost always careful," she retorted.

"Well, at least now we have a time frame," Harry replied, laughing at Alicia and trying to get the plan locked up.

McKenzie ignored the banter, letting it slide, and directed his attention back to Jimmy: "And, of course, a woman's natural curiosity won't be questioned if she wants to look around."

The comment drew him another hostile look from Alicia.

"Yeah, well, curiosity killed the cat, remember?" Pat reminded them.

"But cats have nine lives as I recall," Alicia quipped right back. "Don't worry, cowboy," she said, smiling at the sergeant, "I know plenty of tricks, and I've been in plenty of situations that were more dangerous than this."

Confident that the argument had been put to rest, McKenzie stood up and said: "There's no change in what each of us is doing tomorrow during the day. If Andy is in fact aboard the *Southern Belle*, we still have to find a way to free him. So we need a plan. And we only have three days left in which to do it."

"The other day," Harry began, "I think it was Jimmy . . . brought up the idea of some sort of bait and switch."

"I did?" Jimmy said.

"Yes, you did, Professor," Harry said, giving him an irritated look that said: *Be quiet*. "That idea got me to thinking. We can talk about it later, if you'd like, John."

McKenzie shrugged, saying: "Fine, Harry. So it's settled then. Nothing can proceed any further until Alicia goes aboard the *Southern Belle* and has a look around. But we have confirmed that Edith Edwards exists, and Harry and Alvin plan on following her tomorrow morning. We might have another suspect in this ranch hand, Sanders, who could have a grudge against the senator. Also, we know the man who bought the paper that matches that of the ransom letter was Jason Longwood, and he owns the boat, the *Southern Belle*. And that boat could be the location where Andy is being held. Tomorrow could turn out to be a pretty important day for this investigation, so get some sleep tonight."

* * * * *

The next morning at seven, Harry and Corporal Jones got into the buggy that McKenzie had waiting for them. They headed south, arriving at the Edwards' home long before Edith was expected to leave for the day.

They sat in the buggy for a time as Harry went over their plan.

"We're starting out with very little information, Alvin. We don't know which way she will be traveling, or whether she will be walking or riding," Harry said.

"No, sir, we don't," the corporal concurred.

"But I'm guessing that no matter where she goes, she'll be on the lookout for anybody following her. For all we know, she might be very experienced at this sort of thing."

"I can tell you that she sure seemed calm when she was telling me that pile of horse—uh, horse dung," Alvin said, still angry with himself for being bamboozled by the woman. He stretched out his legs, trying to get comfortable, then added: "So, if she spots us, what do we do?"

"Here's what I'm thinking," Harry told his partner. "The moment she leaves the house, I'll follow her on foot from a safe distance."

"Where will I be?" the soldier asked.

"You're staying with this rig. Listen up, then ask your questions," Harry said, annoyed that Alvin often tried to guess what he was going to say before he had finished speaking.

The corporal slouched in the seat, crossed his arms, and went silent.

"Look, Alvin, as we told you before, this isn't like the army. The object here is to follow her and find out where she goes for the whole day."

"I get it," Alvin replied back. "But you should know, we're pretty stealthy in the army."

"All right," Harry said with a slight smile. "So I walk while you ride in the buggy. If she gets into a coach, then you pick me up, and we follow her. If she stays afoot and I begin to think she suspects me . . . sometimes I can just tell when I've been discovered . . . I'll veer across the street and take off my hat. That will be the signal for you to have the driver stop the buggy, pick me up, and let you out so you can start following her, making sure to keep your head down and covered by that hat of yours as best you can. Then we'll follow you two in the buggy."

"In other words, we're playing that kid's game . . . leapfrog," Jones said, catching on.

"Right, but remember, Alvin, we're going to be cautious frogs . . . Keep your distance, no sudden moves or getting so close that you attract her attention. Don't stare at her, even at her back. Anytime we even suspect she might be onto us, we switch places. And most importantly, act natural, Alvin. Understand?"

"Yes, sir, I do," Corporal Jones replied.

"One last thing, Alvin."

"Yes, sir?"

"Stop calling me sir! My name is Harry!"

When it was eight forty-five, Harry jumped out of the buggy

and had the driver station it around the corner, just out of sight of the Edwards' house. He took a position up the street, sitting on the stone bench where Jones had sat the other day, from which there was a good view of the comings and goings at the house. Harry opened a newspaper he had bought that morning and pretended to read. To the casual observer, it would appear as if he were merely whiling away the time.

At around nine o'clock, the front door to the house opened, and Edith Edwards stepped out. At her appearance, Harry, a pretty decent bird caller, let out with the song of an oriole, which he had whistled for his partner before he had jumped out of the buggy. He thought it was the safest and easiest way to alert Jones. Then he began shadowing the housekeeper, making sure he was undetected. Surprisingly, he managed with all the panache of a true professional.

A brisk walker, Edith Edwards slowed down before stopping at a crossing where a number of wagons, buggies, and horses just kept getting in each other's way. She stood looking up and down the street, which led Harry to believe she was waiting for someone or something. It was a good guess, because a lorry pulled by two tired-looking horses stopped, and Edith Edwards climbed on. The coach moved out, continuing to head north.

Harry waited impatiently for Jones and the buggy to pick him up, cursing under his breath as time seemed to speed up.

Harry told the driver to follow the lorry as he crawled inside. Neither man said anything as the driver stuck with the lorry for a full thirty minutes, slowing to a crawl when it made stops along the way. But Edith Edwards remained on the conveyance even after it turned and headed toward the dock. Finally, after what seemed like hours of tediously avoiding the crowds of people, the lorry pulled to a stop. And to the surprise of both Harry and Alvin, it was here that Edith Edwards disembarked and walked quickly toward a series of piers off to the left, wending her way through the throng of people and hundreds upon hundreds of crates, barrels, and bulging sacks piled high everywhere.

They managed to continue to watch Edith as she crossed over to a long pier where a large paddleboat was anchored. She paused for a moment at the boarding ramp, surveying the people who milled around her, before moving quickly up the ramp and onto the boat.

"Pull up over there," Harry instructed the driver, pointing to a small building.

"What now?" Alvin asked. "We going to board her?"

Harry shook his head. "No, we can't just board it without a reason. No, now we just watch." He gave instructions to the driver, and then the two watched the boat from a distance.

"If the boy's aboard, maybe we could find him ourselves," Corporal Jones suggested, a little too eagerly. "It's a chance I'm willing to take."

"No. We have to assume that whoever planned this has made sure the boy is guarded like the US mint. Besides, if he is on it and if we got caught on the boat, the boy would be moved immediately. Think of it, Alvin, two men storming aboard right now, without knowing any more than we do . . . which is nothing . . . could go horribly wrong, getting us killed, or the boy killed, or maybe all three of us. Also, it's a big boat. Think of this as reconnoitering an enemy position. You'll get your chance for action soon enough, Alvin. I'm pretty sure of that. For now, let's concentrate on watching who comes and goes on that steamboat."

Corporal Jones nodded his head.

"Why don't you regale me with all of your heroic war stories while we watch," Harry suggested, half joking, since he preferred telling stories rather than listening to them.

Harry and Alvin Jones waited and watched, discussing a myriad of topics, but after three hours with no activity to be seen on the boat, the two men decided to position themselves closer to the boat once they found something to eat.

Once they were back and closer to the boat, they could see it had suffered some damage and was in need of repairs. But far more important was its name: *Southern Belle*. Once they saw that, they started talking to the workers to learn what was being said about the boat. They learned that it had been there for at least a month and that it wasn't scheduled to be moved out anytime soon, often adding that it needed a lot of work before it could be sent out.

Finally, sometime around five o'clock, Edith Edwards reappeared. She was alone. She boarded another two-horse coach, which made a wide circle around the area before turning back toward the city.

"We going to follow her again?" Corporal Jones asked.

Harry sighed and nodded. "Yeah, we are. We have to see if Miss Edwards goes straight home. Come on, let's go find a buggy."

Sure enough, the lorry followed a similar route back through the city that it had taken that morning. Very near six o'clock, just as Mrs. Edwards had said, her daughter-in-law arrived back at home.

Harry turned to Jones. "Not very exciting, but most informative, wouldn't you say, Alvin?"

Corporal Jones just shrugged. "If you say so, Harry. If you say so."

"I do. So now let's go back to the hotel and report in."

The corporal told the driver to turn the buggy around and head back to the hotel. Both glanced back for one last look at the Edwards house before traveling out of range.

CHAPTER FOURTEEN

"All right, so here's the plan for tonight to protect Alicia," McKenzie said as Alvin and Harry settled into the settee and chairs in his suite. "I want you to feel free to speak up with any ideas or concerns as we go along. Alicia gets picked up at eight. That gives us a little less than two hours to prepare.

"Pat, I want you on the dock no later than . . . say, seven forty-five, scouting the area and taking note of anyone arriving or leaving the paddle wheel. Blend in as best you can, but I want you to determine the number of men on the boat, the points of entry and retreat, and locations where we could bottleneck or ambush them."

Nelson nodded silently. He had done this sort of thing many times over the years.

"Harry, I want you down at the waterfront too, but you keep your eyes and ears open for anything at all that might be useful, anything. Also, if something happens on the boat, Harry, you get to Pat as fast as you can."

"What will I be doing, sir?" Corporal Jones asked.

"You'll be out in a boat with Jimmy," McKenzie answered.

"I beg your pardon, sir?" Jones said, while Jimmy squawked: "What?"

McKenzie put the two men straight. "I want you to take a boat around the side of the boat that we can't see. Allan has arranged for a boat to be ready for you just south of the *Southern Belle*. I want to know if there are other any means of getting onto or off the boat by water. Anything at all that could be used by them or us. You'll also be alert in case Alicia gets in trouble and has to jump ship. Any questions?"

"None," said Jimmy, looking sullen.

Corporal Jones eyed the others before asking: "Are we going to be bringing the authorities in on this? You know . . . the police or the military?"

McKenzie shook his head. "Corporal, in this case we are the authorities. So the answer is no, we cannot get the police or the army involved for a number of reasons, the most important being that we don't want to tip our hand too soon and jeopardize our chances of saving Andy. It's best for you to just follow my orders."

"Yes, sir," Jones said, even though he didn't really understand.

"I don't believe Longwood will hurt Alicia," McKenzie said, "but I do want to be prepared for any eventuality.

Alicia entered the room.

Harry's jaw dropped when he saw Alicia in an emerald-green gown. "Holy smoke," he barely got out.

"Wow, Ali!" Nelson added.

"Alicia, good, you're here," McKenzie said, taking a professional tone. "We were going over things for tonight." He told her where the agents would be positioned, then said to her: "I think you should take some kind of weapon when you go tonight."

"I've got my knife, the derringer, which I usually keep in my purse," she enumerated. "And there's the fan."

"I'm not sure it's smart to carry a gun in your purse while

you're around a person like Longwood. But I do think you should take the fan."

"Do we know what kind of person Jason Longwood is, John? After all . . . wait a minute . . . are you afraid Jason might try to get fresh with me? Not jealous are you?" She was having fun, trying to provoke him. She knew it was not the time to do so, but she had given much thought to the fact that he had been so adamant that she join Longwood for dinner and that they weren't a couple the previous day, that she wanted to get back at him.

McKenzie was thrown off by her questions. In fact, even though he rarely blushed, when she asked if he was jealous, he could feel the heat rising to his cheeks. Fortunately for him, Harry quickly made a joke, which gave him time to regain his composure.

"Well, we can rehearse if you want, Alicia," Harry said. "I'll be Jason."

The others laughed, until they realized Alicia wasn't laughing.

"I've had plenty of practice fending off men, Harry," she said. "I can take care of myself."

She shot them all a look of disappointment before leaving the room, not even bothering to close the door behind her.

McKenzie called out: "Meeting tomorrow morning at seven right here." To the men: "Time to get to work!"

Alicia hadn't been gone long, when there was a knock at the door. Jimmy cautiously opened the door a few inches. A hotel bellhop gave a small deferential bow before handing a note addressed to Alicia.

"For Miss Faye," the bellhop said through dry lips. The young man had seen Alicia in the hotel a number of times since her arrival, and he thought she was the most beautiful woman he had ever seen.

Harry stepped forward to tip the bellboy, but McKenzie,

well aware of Howser's little pocket-picking trick, jumped in, securing a coin from his pocket and extending his hand faster than did the magician.

"Thank you," he said. "We'll make sure she gets this." He closed the door and listened to make sure the young man had actually left. He gave an all clear sign.

"I'm taking this to Ali, while you head to your stations," McKenzie said, and note in hand, he headed to Alicia's room where he knocked softly.

* * * * *

Alicia answered the door and stepped aside to let McKenzie enter. She moved over to a chair, but just stood there.

"Harry wanted me to tell you to break a leg, Ali," he said as she continued to stare. "Alicia . . ." McKenzie started to say, but Alicia wouldn't let him finish.

"I know, John, I'll be careful. But I need a little time alone." When he nodded and turned, she grabbed his hand, looked up into his eyes, and, standing on her tiptoes, she gave him a kiss on the cheek, which startled McKenzie.

"Remember that Alvin and Jimmy will have a boat out in the water, so if you get into real trouble, scream and jump overboard. And if you jump in, make a lot of noise so they can get to you quickly."

"If I have to jump, they better hurry," she said. "I'll be making plenty a noise, since I can't swim. Don't say anything. Just go."

"I almost forgot . . . this came for you," he said, handing her the envelope. As she looked down at it, he reached out to touch her check, but stopped himself. He wished her luck, then he left the room.

* * * * *

"It's a beautiful evening, don't you think?" Alicia said to Jason Longwood as they boarded the *Southern Belle*. She stopped about two-thirds up the boarding ramp as if to look at the view of the water, when in fact she was hoping to catch a glimpse of Jones and Jimmy in the boat, even though she knew they would not venture that close to the paddleboat.

"Only made more so by your ravishing presence," Longwood said, smiling.

"Why, Mr. Longwood, you are a charmer, aren't you?" Alicia said, holding her fan in her hand. *Or at least for now*, she thought to herself. Still, it wasn't all an act. He might turn out to be a ruthless kidnapper, but there was no doubting his swarthy good looks and attentive manner.

"Please, call me Jason," he told her as he led her up the remainder of the ramp. "I insist."

"Fine, but only if you call me Alicia," she said, tipping her head up at him and smiling. "So . . . Jason, this is a remarkable boat. I'd love to see every inch of her."

"I thought perhaps a quiet dinner in the main hall first with a small band to entertain us. And this time, I promise, you will not be imposed upon to sing."

"You're referring to the social club?" she remarked. "Actually, I didn't mind. It was very flattering."

Longwood shook his head. "I assure you, no one enjoyed it more than I, but still, it was an imposition. So," he rubbed his palms together, "no such demands tonight. This evening we shall dine in peaceful solitude while you and I are entertained."

"Sounds perfect. But don't wait too long to show off the *Southern Belle*," Alicia suggested. "It's rare that one gets to enjoy a vessel when it's basically empty. Without all the people and fuss, it's much more relaxing. Nonetheless, I must remind you that I do have a curfew."

Longwood seemed slightly perturbed at her comment; Alicia could see his jaw clench.

"I'm looking forward to this evening." This time Alicia didn't press the point about touring the boat, as doing so might arouse his suspicion.

Longwood took her arm in his to escort her across the deck to a wide set of double doors that opened into the main dining room. There was room for perhaps seventy-five diners, with a stage up front for those who wished to dance. To Alicia the room seemed cavernous with only a couple of waiters, the musicians, and the sound of cooks working in the kitchen. Jason escorted Alicia to one of the tables near the front of the hall and held a chair out for her.

Two white-clad waiters appeared tableside as if by magic, bringing over two flutes and a polished ice bucket. One stepped back as the other poured the champagne.

Alicia took one of the glasses and held it up.

"To a brighter future," she toasted.

"May the South rise again," Jason added, tipping his glass toward hers.

"Hear, hear," she said and sipped the champagne. "How in the world did you manage to get hold of this excellent champagne from those thieving Northerners?"

"Among my many ventures, I am an importer and exporter of various commodities, including spirits and fine wines. Until the Yankee blockade, that is," Jason stated almost in a hiss, but then he smiled at Alicia. "In spite of everything, I managed to keep a couple of warehouses where I stored enough of an inventory to more than meet my needs for quite some time. But keeping the *Belle* was what was most important to me, and I managed to do it," he added with pride.

Alicia glanced around the room, and Longwood gestured to the band to begin the music.

"Alicia, you should have seen her in her heyday. She was the queen of the Mississippi River, but as the war raged on, I was forced to lend her out to the military. Then toward the end of the war, she was damaged by Federal artillery. And now she's docked here while I wait for a crew to repair her."

"Is that what you did during the conflict, Jason? Were you in the navy?" Alicia asked. She hoped that it wouldn't seem as though she were prying, but rather expressing interest in him and his background.

Longwood shook his head and then waved to a waiter, indicating the meal should begin. She could see he was used to being in control of his surroundings.

"No, not the navy, but I did serve," he said. "Because of my background in commerce, I was assigned to the Quartermaster Corps. I was in charge of logistics for this region."

She waved her fan coyly. "Gracious, whatever did that entail? Quarter logistical, did you say?"

Longwood laughed and patted her free hand. "No, my dear, Quartermaster Corps, in charge of logistics. Inventory control, and distribution of supplies such as uniforms, weaponry, tents, and the like for our gallant boys at the front," he explained. "Toward the end I had to use the *Southern Belle* as a transport."

"My, you certainly gave a lot for our beloved South, didn't you?"

Longwood looked down. "Not as much as my brother," he commented bitterly. "I lost him at Gettysburg. Then both my parents perished shortly after our plantation back home was ransacked and destroyed. It seems so long ago now." He looked back up into her eyes. "But let's not talk of such things."

A bowl of fragrant, creamed soup was placed in front of them. "I managed to rescue the best chef south of the Mason-Dixon Line and brought him here with me. I told him I would have him keelhauled if he didn't prepare a meal fit for someone as special as you."

"I am left breathless by your flattery, kind sir," Alicia said, walking that fine line between leading him on and fending him off. She had a mission to accomplish and had to get through this evening with her motive undetected.

After the dinner filled with one extravagant course after another, Jason stood and held out his hand to Alicia. "It's been too long since I've waltzed with such a lovely companion," he said.

"Jason, you must tell the chef he is more than safe from . . . what did you call it . . . being keelhauled? And while it was all perfectly delicious, would you mind terribly if we took a stroll around before we dance." She touched his arm. "The meal, though delectable, was rather abundant, and with certain foods often in short supply, I must confess I haven't eaten so much in a very long time," she explained.

An expression of concern spread across his face again. His eyes went from smiling to black in an instant. Alicia was becoming more convinced he was concealing something on the steamboat.

Jason cleared his throat and nodded. "But of course. Just ignore those things that are in need of repair."

I'll bet that ransom money would go a long way toward fixing that, Alicia thought to herself. She had discovered a motive.

Longwood took her by the hand a bit too forcefully. "We'll go to the upper deck first."

Grabbing his arm, she laughed. "Oh, don't be so predictable. We have all evening to look at the stars and dance. For now I want to have a look around. You know, I have always been fascinated by architecture, especially hotels . . . probably having stayed in so many. Now that I'm walking around, I realize boats are like floating hotels. I know it sounds silly, but I've never been on a boat like this one. So, Jason, show me around, and then we can finish up top with that dance." When she wanted something, Alicia Faye was a hard one to refuse.

"Very well, then. So be it," he replied reluctantly. "We shall go up top later," Longwood said, clearing his throat.

As the pair walked, Longwood seemed to relax a little. "The *Belle* is a stern-wheeler, meaning she is powered from behind," Jason began to explain. "They also make side-wheelers that are similar, just wider. I hope to own one someday." He stopped and patted her arm. "All in good time."

"Of course," Alicia replied sweetly. "I'm sure you will."

They came to stairwell leading below, with a burnished wood railing.

"This is the cabin deck," Jason explained as they descended. "These are the rooms used when we carry passengers, who can afford a bit of extra comfort and privacy."

Alicia stopped to open a door and peek in, watching Longwood's reaction as she did so. Longwood didn't seem bothered in the least, which puzzled her. *If he is hiding a kidnapped boy, he's not acting like it now.*

"I see these rooms all have familiar names, like Texas or Alabama," Alicia said.

"Yes. They're staterooms."

Alicia didn't react, just commented: "Well, they are rather generous in size."

Longwood shook his head and laughed. "No, my dear. The custom of calling large hotel rooms staterooms actually started some years back on Mississippi paddleboats, when they began naming their guest cabins after states . . . Tennessee or Georgia. Thus the term . . . staterooms."

Alicia laughed too, opening and waving her fan. "Well, you certainly do learn something new every day, I swear."

Longwood squeezed her arm as they descended another stairway. This level, however, was a large open area. At the present time, it was empty except for a few hammocks strung between posts. As they walked along in silence for several minutes, Alicia looked over at her companion, hoping he would resume talking, for she was beginning to feel nervous.

Finally, Jason turned and spread his arms, stating: "This is the transportation deck. Not much to see here now. But, when she's running the river, this is where we put the cargo."

When they reached the end of the deck, there was yet another stairway, though narrower. The entry to it, unlike the others, was secured with a chain. A burly man came into Alicia's view, leaning against the wall near a door, looking very much as if he were guarding something . . . or someone.

"What's down there, Jason?" Alicia asked. Out of the corner of her eye, she could see the guard was trying to hide a gun at his side, which he did unsuccessfully since Alicia prided herself on her observational skills.

"Oh, the engines, the machinery that powers the boat," he answered.

"Oh, let's go down and look," Alicia urged.

Once again, Longwood's expression changed just enough for Alicia to see that she had touched a nerve. "I'm afraid I cannot allow that, Alicia. It is far too dirty a place for you to go in . . . dressed as you are. More importantly, it's dangerous . . . There's the steam-powered engine, boilers, all types of machinery even I don't understand." He took her arm. "You wouldn't believe the stories I've heard about . . . What am I saying . . . that's not a topic for an evening as pleasurable as this one."

Not one to be deterred, she kept on. "Please, I would love to see it. My father was a railroad engineer, and I'm fascinated by machinery. I don't mind a little grease, truly I don't," she said, in spite of the fact that the dress had been borrowed.

"I am sorry, my dear, Alicia, but it's out of the question," Jason replied, but there was an edge to his tone.

"Even if I asked extra nicely?" Alicia asked.

"Some other time, perhaps," Longwood said abruptly. He took hold of her arms and turned her back in the direction they had come. His touch was no longer gentle, and she feared he might actually rip her dress. Still, she chose to ignore his rising temper.

"All right, if you insist, Jason. Shall we go up top and dance instead?" Alicia said in such a way as to suggest she might be keen on his more brutish ways.

Jason immediately relaxed, and he escorted her topside, patting her hand and making small talk as they went back up.

They danced on the upper deck and shared an after-dinner liqueur. During what must have been the fourth song they danced to, Jason leaned in and kissed Alicia's neck, and she knew she had to put an end to the evening. So she laughed and pulled her head back, waiting until the song finished before saying goodnight.

"Jason, I have had a perfectly wonderful evening, but I don't want to spoil it. Would you please arrange for the carriage to take me back to the hotel?"

Jason leaned in closer. "You know you are breaking my heart, don't you?"

Alicia opened her fan and waved it.

"I'd like to see you again, if I may, Jason," she said, tightening her shawl before turning to leave, certain there would be an invitation forthcoming.

"Certainly," he said and escorted her off the boat.

At the carriage, Longwood said goodnight, and he leaned

in to kiss her. Alicia stepped back and gave him her hand to kiss, smiling at him and fanning herself, before climbing inside.

On the ride back to the hotel, thoughts were rushing through her head. *Andy has to be on the boat. And he's still alive, because why else would you station guards around if he wasn't? There doesn't seem to be anything else on board to protect. Don't trust Longwood, Ali. He's a ruthless man who is only interested in power and money. Unless they move Andy, I think I know where they're keeping him.*

CHAPTER FIFTEEN

By seven the following morning, the agents, with the exception of Alicia and Jimmy, had assembled in McKenzie's suite. The night before, upon returning from the *Southern Belle*, Alicia had gone to John's room to tell him what she had discovered on the boat. McKenzie had listened intently as she enumerated the reasons why she believed Andy was on the boat. She told him she was tired, so she thought she might not make it to the meeting until eight.

Now McKenzie relayed the information to Harry, Patrick, and Corporal Jones. After discussing it, and with only a few days left before the deadline for the ransom payment, they decided to move ahead and make a plan.

Nelson described the layout of the area around the *Southern Belle*—the boarding ramps, nearby boats, possible escape routes, as well as the locations of the cargo waiting to be loaded, unloaded, or bartered for by local merchants in the vicinity. Before he had finished, Jimmy burst into the room.

"You aren't going . . . to believe what . . . I've got for us," he could barely get out as he stood there, gasping and panting.

He motioned with his hand and, finally able to talk, said: "Pull that table out from the wall, so we can all get around it." He produced a tube the length of his arm from which he pulled out another tube. He smiled at the others and then asked for Alvin's help while he unrolled the top piece on the roll as the others guessed what it could be, settling on a map. It was a map of sorts, but it was sketched on a piece of cloth. It had been drawn by a sailor, recovering from a broken leg, a couple of years back. He sat on the dock every day, sketching in great detail what he saw.

No one said anything as they studied the amateur's map while Jimmy began unrolling the remaining tube, which revealed itself to be a blueprint of a boat.

"Is this the *Southern Belle*?" Pat asked.

"It isn't the *Belle*, but the boat builder I met with said it's as close as you can get," Jimmy said.

"Nice job, Professor," Harry said, favorably impressed with the scientist's inquisitive mind and quick thinking.

While studying the blueprint, McKenzie asked: "How did you get this, Jimmy, and when?"

"Well, once I learned that Jason Longwood owned a paddleboat that was docked locally, I tracked down the oldest boat builder still in business after twenty-three years. I went to see him this morning. He knew all about the paddleboat's design and was able to supply me with this blueprint. Changes were made here and there on the *Belle*, but not the basic size or design."

Harry scratched his head. "And he was willing to just give up this information up?"

Jimmy shook his head. "No, not at first. I told him I was an apprentice attorney and that I had a client interested in building a paddleboat to start up a business now that the war was over. I said my client had seen a boat along the river called the *Southern*

Belle that he admired and that he sent me to gather information about its construction, the costs involved, and so on."

"Alicia believes the boy is probably being kept somewhere near the engine room, but there's a lot of area to cover to get to him," Harry commented.

Jimmy pointed to a place on the drawing. "If you notice, there is a small room here on the lower deck. I saw it when the builder first showed me the blueprint. My guess is it's a personal cabin for the engine room chief. Regardless, that cabin would make an excellent place to stash the lad at night so he doesn't go wandering around and get himself hurt."

"Makes sense," Pat agreed.

"I think you're right about them keeping Andy locked up tight at night, Jimmy," McKenzie said. "But remember, this is still guesswork on our part. He might not even be there."

"So you don't trust Alicia?" Pat asked.

"I do trust her," he said. "But I'm going to go over to see Allan, I need to talk this over with him. I want you to stay here and start coming up with a plan to go after the boy the night before the deadline is up."

* * * * *

Once McKenzie apprised Allan of all they had learned over the last number of days, Pinkerton didn't need to be convinced that they should move ahead with a plan. McKenzie was back at his suite before ten thirty to let the others know.

Harry, Jimmy, and Pat had been brainstorming, and they outlined for him how they thought the rescue should be carried out. They also said they had a lot to get done before it could happen.

Corporal Jones told them at the present, the river side of the boat was damaged and that it could not be used for the rescue even if they had a boat ready nearby.

"I honestly think that taking into account the boy's safety, the speed necessary for a quick exit, and the potential danger we're up against, any escape by water would be impossible. You'd have to either lower him by rope with someone holding onto him or throw him into the river and hope we can recover the boy before he drowns," he explained. "And all the while, men on the boat would be shooting at him at you."

"So we're back to boarding and exiting from dockside," McKenzie muttered.

"Yeah, I'm afraid so," Jones confirmed.

"What about you, Pat, what do you think, since our biggest challenge will be getting the boy off the boat?" McKenzie asked.

"Well, as I've said before, I'm a believer in a full-on ambush, using snipers as backup, but with a child involved . . . well, it's just too dangerous. So we think the best way would be having two men sneaking on board to get Andy. One of those two would be you . . . being as how you are similar in build and height with Longwood, which could come in handy. Since we now know there's no way off the boat except by using the ramp, once we have Andy, we should probably create some sort of distraction to get the attention of the guards and anyone else on the boat. Maybe a feint attack, coupled with a rear guard action after the boy is off the boat. Something along those lines," Pat said.

"I think I have an idea that could help once the boy is off the boat, John," Harry inserted the second Pat finished talking. "I've sent a message to Abe Hamilton . . . the fellow helping out down-on-their-luck entertainers, you remember . . . If he can locate the prop I need, I think I can pull off the perfect bait-and-switch trick. And good news . . . I know just the person here in town who could help me do it."

Alicia offered her opinion. "Well, that sort of thing seems right in line with your area of expertise, Harry . . . illusion and misdirection."

"Thanks, Ali," Harry said with a smile. "Nothing like putting the success or the failure of this operation on me."

"Harry, maybe Alicia's got something there," McKenzie said, stroking his chin in thought. "When we have time later, why don't you partner with Jimmy and come up with that distraction we need while you're waiting to hear back from Hamilton? I'm not going to even ask you what the prop is until you're sure you can get it. But let me know the minute you find that out."

"Our success hinges on finding him fast," Pat repeated.

"Yes, it does," McKenzie agreed. "For now, get out of here and do what you need to do. In the meantime, I'm going over the blueprint of the boat with Alicia, if that's all right with her."

"Not a problem, John."

* * * * *

Pat Nelson headed down to the docks, dressed as a longshoreman, in order to assess the best way to attack the *Southern Belle.* He tried to blend in, but there was one burly, ape-shaped fellow, who looked to be in charge of the area, keeping a close eye on him. Whenever the man started walking toward him, Nelson would hoist a burlap bag on his shoulder to cover his face while he tried to melt in among the other dockworkers. Toward the late afternoon, when he saw activity on the *Belle*, he hid behind some crates to watch. It turned out to be a loose nail on a ramp, which was easily fixed with a bit of hammering.

Because Harry had been insistent, Nelson wrote down the approximate dimensions of the largest crates. He also copied down any names and markings on them.

Meanwhile, Jimmy was off on a search for any information he could ferret out on Longwood and his businesses. He was joined by Corporal Jones.

Harry was busy, putting together the most important trick he had ever attempted, which began by looking up an old acquaintance.

* * * * *

The agents met in McKenzie's suite the following morning to discuss strategies. Notations, lines, and arrows were being added to the map of the dock area and on the ship blueprint. Harry arrived late. He had gotten good news from Hamilton, and he had located his friend, Mickey Dunn, who was going to be showing up at the suite as soon as he finished running an errand for Harry.

Harry took McKenzie into the bedroom to talk, leaving the door ajar. He quickly outlined the plan that he and Mickey had worked out.

"You're sure you and Mickey can do this, Harry?" McKenzie asked, even though he didn't have an alternative plan in mind and he didn't know Mickey Dunn, hadn't even heard Harry mention him before.

When there was a knock at the door, McKenzie stuck his head out and gestured for Jimmy to get it.

"As long as we can get our prop in place," Harry explained once he had McKenzie's attention again. "It's due to arrive by train tomorrow," Harry told him, but seeing hesitation in John's eyes, he added: "I trust Mickey, John. We go back many years. I'd trust him with my life under almost any circumstances."

"Almost any?" said a voice from outside the bedroom door.

Harry laughed as McKenzie pushed the door open to look

into the sitting room. Patrick, Jimmy, and Corporal Jones were staring, still as statues, their eyes wide with surprise.

"Mickey Dunn at your service," said Harry's friend, extending his hand to McKenzie.

McKenzie slowly lowered his gaze when Dunn repeated his name. He took Dunn's hand hesitantly, for it was half the size of his own, being that Dunn was a midget.

Harry then introduced Mickey to the rest of the team, who had luckily recovered somewhat from their initial shock.

"Say, is this on the level, or is it another of your cons, Harry?" Mickey asked, getting uncomfortable with all eyes on him, but still checking out the swanky suite.

"I can assure you it is, Mr. Dunn," McKenzie said.

"Call me Mickey."

"All right, Mickey, what has Harry told you about what we're doing here?" the chief agent asked.

"Nothing, except what he expects me to do and that we're doing it to rescue some kid," Dunn said, pulling a cigar from his pocket. "You mind?" he asked, lighting up before anyone could reply. "That's all I know."

"Good, and let's keep it that way. No need for you to know any more. So, do you have any concerns about your part in the operation?" McKenzie asked.

"Not yet," Mickey said.

"It will be dangerous . . . no question," McKenzie informed Dunn. "But we are very good at what we do, and we always do everything we can to avoid violence, but, if I'm being honest, there is bound to be shooting. I just don't know how much. What I do know is that Harry says your help on this is essential for our plan to work."

"Mickey, you know this trick like the back of your hand," Harry said. "We've all done a variation of it over the years. The only difference here is that the audience may try to shoot at us . . . with bullets, not tomatoes."

"Us . . . or me, Harry?"

"Any one of us," Nelson stated without further comment.

"Are you in this with us?" McKenzie asked. "Of course, you'll receive payment for your assistance."

Alicia walked into the room, and Mickey Dunn's mouth dropped open. "I'll be damned," he said. "Alicia Faye, the Queen of the South herself." He walked over to her and gave her a hug. "Ali, my girl, looking as good as ever! How do you do it?"

"It's good to see you again, Mickey," Alicia said, looking genuinely happy to see him, and it wasn't missed by McKenzie. She now held his hand in her own as she explained to the others: "From time to time over the years . . . and depending on the show . . . Mickey and I have traveled in the same circle. Often with Harry"—her eyes met Harry's—"right, Howser?"

"Yeah, he was always getting in the way," Mickey joked.

"Hey, knock it off," Harry protested.

"Now, Mickey, you know you were always first in my heart," Alicia said with a wink. "It's just that it wasn't meant to be." She let go of his hand and made a perfect curtsy.

"Said Helen of Troy as she turned her back on the Greeks," Mickey retorted. "Ali, please tell me you aren't a Pink too?"

"Am and have been for some years now," she replied. "But keep that to yourself, all right?"

After a few more minutes of joking and talking, McKenzie repeated: "So, Mickey, can we count on you? I'd like to give you some time to think about it, but we're short on that as it is."

"You don't have to say no more," Mickey said, taking his stinky cigar out of his mouth. "I could be glib and say I'll stay simply because Alicia is here, and that wouldn't be too much of a lie, but the truth is, I was in the minute Harry mentioned the kid. I feel mighty bad for the kid's folks." Mickey paused to puff on his big stogie and blow a few smoke rings, before adding: "There ain't been much sideshow work lately, and I know times is tough. But kidnapping a kid now . . . that's low. I hope we get to deal out some justice. Yeah, count me in."

"All right," McKenzie said. "Let's go over the boat's layout once again. Now's the time to make any modifications to the plan, keeping in mind anything new we've learned."

Nelson was pointing out a location on the map, when Harry, Jimmy, and Mickey backed away from the table and began whispering. After several minutes, Harry stepped back to the table and pointed to a place on the map.

"This is where it has to happen. You figure out a way to get Andy off the boat, and Mickey and I will make sure he stays safe till we can get him back to his family. Jimmy and Alvin, we may need your help when our prop arrives tomorrow."

Again a knock sounded at the door, and this time McKenzie answered. A bellhop handed him an envelope with a return address of Albert Peterson, an alias used by Allan Pinkerton to avoid revealing the identify of his agents.

"What is it, John?" Harry asked while Jimmy tried to peer over the chief's shoulder.

McKenzie gave Jimmy a pesky look; he held the photograph of Andy in his hand. "This is a copy of the photograph of Andy that the Secret Service took to examine," he explained. "Harry come over and look at this."

Harry had asked McKenzie to get the photo, and now he took it over by the window. "Obviously they bought these clothes after they kidnapped him from his bed," Harry said, looking at the clothes Andy was wearing. "I wish I knew what color they were and where they got them."

"So you foresee problems?" McKenzie asked.

"No," Harry said after a moment's consideration. "In fact, it's probably better this way." He turned to face Mickey. "I need you to find a store or a tailor who can put together the same or a similar set of clothes in the next twenty-four hours. I'm going to cut Andy's head off in this photo so you can take it along."

"This ought to cover it, but let me know if you need more," McKenzie said as he counted out more than enough money to cover the cost.

"If everybody tells you it can't be done in time, then find me two identical overcoats," Harry told Mickey.

"We'll also need to have a closed carriage, capable of some speed," McKenzie told Pat. "Arrange to pick it up tomorrow, and tell them we'll need it through the weekend. That way there should be no mix-ups. Harry, I know I already asked, but can you and Mickey be ready in time?"

Harry looked at Mickey Dunn, who was sitting, puffing his cigar.

"Don't see a problem, Harry," said Mickey, flicking a good inch of ash on the rug. "Should be fine. It's nothing we haven't done before."

"Corporal Jones, over the next two days you'll be working along with Jimmy, helping Harry and Mickey out whenever you are needed."

Corporal Jones nodded his head, but he kept flashing looks at Harry and Mickey as though he didn't trust them and whatever they were cooking up.

Harry turned to McKenzie and smiled. "There you have it."

Corporal Jones still hadn't been filled in on a lot of the specifics, and he couldn't help but feel inadequate around this group of professionals. He preferred military tactics over the handiwork of a magician. "What part exactly am I doing in this?" he asked McKenzie. "Don't I get to go in on the assault with Nelson like you promised?"

It was Harry who shook his head and laughed, saying: "No, once we start the plan, you'll be staying in one place. But you will be back in uniform."

The corporal didn't feel any better about his role than he had before he asked his question.

"That's it then. Two days from now . . . in the evening," McKenzie announced. "That's when we go in."

CHAPTER SIXTEEN

The team was a flurry of busyness as they went about getting the legwork done and conferring about the details, the timing, and the unknowns. McKenzie stayed at the hotel, working on a timeline as he took everything they had learned into consideration.

Harry went down to the docks with Jimmy and Alvin in preparation for the arrival and placement of the prop. There they made contact with one of Mickey's friends named Marv Morgan, who, for a small price, was willing to keep his mouth shut as well as help them out in procuring a dray and the men needed to pick up and haul the prop. Marv had three of the biggest men Harry had ever seen work with him moving, shifting, and restacking crates near the *Belle*. Each of the trio was given a few extra coins, which Harry didn't even try to filch, to stay until after dark to move the prop into place once it was arrived in the dray.

Mickey, with Alicia's help, had found a tailor who could produce the needed clothing in the allotted time. Then he sent them to a store where they could purchase the shirt Andy was wearing in the photograph.

The agents kept McKenzie up to date on everything they were doing, which led to additional modifications to their plan.

* * * * *

When Alvin Jones arrived at the suite that night to find out if there was anything else he could do, McKenzie asked him to take a seat.

"The prop's going into position tonight. That's where Harry is . . . down at the dock waiting for it to be hauled in, Captain. We'll be ready for tomorrow night," Alvin blurted out as McKenzie poured himself a drink.

"That's good to hear, Corporal," McKenzie said, asking Alvin if he was interested in a drink by lifting the bottle of whiskey toward him and tilting his head.

"None for me, thanks, Captain."

"Corporal, I don't know what Harry has told you or what you've gleaned from our meetings, but you will be playing a most important role come tomorrow night," McKenzie said, easing into a chair and taking a sip from his glass. "Do you have your uniform with you?"

"Yes, sir, I do. And Harry's told me I will be with Andy once he's rescued."

"That's right. If we are correct that Andy is, in fact, on the boat, when we find him and get him off the boat, he'll be scared. You're the only one of us he will recognize, and wearing the uniform will help in all the confusion he'll be experiencing. We're counting on you to help him through this. But take my advice, and leave the saber behind."

"With pleasure, sir," said Alvin. "Never used it once in the whole lousy war. Damned things ought to be cut down and made into whittling knives. Then maybe they'd be good for something."

Sergeant Nelson had entered the room midway through the conversation. "You're right, Corporal. A military doctor once told me that he could count the number of sword wounds he treated over the course of the war on one hand."

"All right then," McKenzie said as he stood up. "Off you go, Alvin. See you in the morning."

"Goodnight, sir," the corporal said, pushing himself up and out of the chair. He left the room quietly.

"Have a drink, Pat, and freshen mine while you're at it," McKenzie said, handing his glass to Nelson.

"We've arranged to get the buggy Jimmy will be driving first thing in the morning," Nelson told McKenzie, pouring a drink for himself and topping off John's.

"Do you think we'll be able to pull this off, Pat?" McKenzie asked soberly, taking the glass from Patrick and lifting it in a toast to his long-time friend.

"I hope to God we can," Nelson said, and threw back his whiskey before heading to his room. "See you bright and early, John."

* * * * *

The following morning they gathered to go over the timing of the plan one last time. McKenzie had worked at it all night, and he believed nothing had been overlooked.

"One last time, then," McKenzie said, turning to Jimmy. "We've already arranged for the buggy you'll be driving, so you'll need to have that in position by six."

"Got it," Jimmy replied.

"Mickey and Alvin, I want you in position two hours before we board the *Southern Belle*."

"Yes, sir!" Alvin Jones said loudly, snapping to attention, while Mickey was lighting up another of his cigars.

"We board at seven o'clock," Pat announced.

"Shouldn't we go under cover of darkness?" Alvin asked.

"I'll admit it would probably work in our favor, but I need the light to get Andy off the boat and to shore safely," said Harry. "And if this is going to work, we need anyone pursuing us to see us."

While Harry was talking, Alicia was looking over McKenzie's notes as well as the maps. She stood up, clearing her throat loudly to get everyone's attention. "I don't see what I'm going to do on any of these papers," she said with irritation at McKenzie. "You originally had me going . . ."

McKenzie didn't let her finish, but he refused to look at her. "As soon as we finish here, you're heading out to Senator Schurz's ranch. Allan has a carriage waiting for you outside already and . . ."

This time it was Alicia who wouldn't let him finish. "And exactly what am I supposed do at the ranch?" she asked defiantly.

"Allan Pinkerton is waiting there. He wanted to be kept up to date, and now that everyone knows their part in the rescue, I want you to fill him in," McKenzie told Alicia. "I need you to deliver those papers in your hands as well . . . the ones marked Allan," John said, walking over and gathering up the papers and sticking them in an envelope as he motioned for her to come over to the map. "This is far too important and complicated to explain to him in a letter. See here . . . that's the escape route we will be taking. Tell Allan we need at least ten of his most trusted men, here in St. Louis, to meet here and help us out in any gunfight." He pointed to the spot on the map, pausing to make sure Alicia saw precisely where he was pointing. "I'll also want agents available to round up any men left on the *Southern Belle* once the fight is over." He didn't add the words "still alive."

Alicia nodded, even though she was still miffed at being left out of the action. "Yes, I understand, John."

McKenzie knew she was unhappy with the change in the plan, and he wouldn't put it past her to ignore his order. "Alicia, you are not to go on board the *Belle* again under any circumstances. We don't know where Longwood will be when we attack, and I do not want you anywhere on or near that boat when the fighting breaks out. Is that understood?"

"I can take care of myself," she replied haughtily.

"I'm sure you can," McKenzie snapped. "But that isn't the point. There is still the possibility that the boy is not on board, and in that case, you may have to renew your acquaintance with Longwood. It won't do to have you seen with a group of Yankee detectives in tow."

"Yes, I understand," she replied, adding: "You think because I'm a woman, I have to be protected from Jason."

McKenzie bristled at her use of Longwood's Christian name.

"You know I can be used to distract him," she reminded him. "It wouldn't be hard even to keep him away from the *Belle*, if need be."

Harry chimed in: "If anyone can, it's you, Alicia."

When McKenzie failed to respond, Alicia moved over to him, forcing him to look her in her eyes. "Don't push me to the side . . . not when we're so close to getting Andy."

"It's too dangerous, Alicia. If he should go to trial, we'll need your testimony. We'll need you alive." McKenzie tried to make her understand, even scare her, but she wasn't having it.

"Is that really it, John? We've been putting ourselves in harm's way for years, so what's changed now? You know what I'm capable of doing." Alicia refused to back down.

McKenzie knew what had changed. He had. It was bad enough she had spent one evening with Jason Longwood. He wanted to keep her alive and healthy, if not for the agency, then for himself.

"If you're on that boat, the boy won't be the only one we'll have to save. Besides, you could be putting everyone at risk."

In spite of the awkwardness of the situation, Nelson finally spoke up: "We're already at risk, John, and you know we wouldn't let anything happen to her." He paused to put his hand up so he could finish, sensing an argument might be coming. "Alicia's right. Longwood needs to be kept away from his boat."

"Let me take care of him, John," Alicia said, a pleading edge to her voice she tried to tamp down.

McKenzie took a few minutes to think, pacing back and forth in front of the others.

"All right, but you keep him away from the *Belle*," he finally said, having no arguments left. "Do you think you can find him?"

"I believe I can," she answered, as she stood there trying to figure out where she could find him.

"Make sure you have a weapon with you," Pat reminded her, feeling somewhat responsible for her involvement.

"Remember, everyone, unless we are fired upon or attacked with deadly intent, I want to try to avoid killing anyone. No shooting unless we are fired upon," McKenzie said. "And because we're not 100 percent sure that Andy is on the *Belle*, I don't want anyone to be accused of cold-blooded murder if we shoot someone."

"And once we have the boy?" Jimmy asked.

"If we confirm that Longwood is responsible for the kidnapping and we have the boy . . . we do what it takes to get him home safely." McKenzie paused to let that sink in, then: "We meet back here at four, which gives you time to take care of anything you might have missed. And, for the boy's sake, good luck to us all."

CHAPTER SEVENTEEN

Working well into the afternoon, McKenzie's team members were in positions by six that evening. A stormy sky had them all worried, but as the seven o'clock hour drew near, the clouds began to break up slowly. The dock had quieted down, the workers near the *Belle* sent home for the day, thanks to Marv, who had concocted some sort of cock-and-bull story to hasten their departure.

It was assumed Alicia had managed to find Longwood, since he hadn't shown his face from the time the team had taken up their positions. However, a number of armed men had been spotted, carrying guns as they patrolled the boat.

McKenzie and Harry waited on the dock, concealed behind the cargo stacked double near Longwood's paddleboat. McKenzie was the only one dressed in a suit and coat, armed with his cane and a gun. Harry was dressed in dark brown, head to toe.

"Let's hope Pat can get into position without being noticed," Harry said in a whisper.

"If anyone can, it's Nelson," McKenzie said.

Almost simultaneously with their comments, there was a barely perceptible *clank* which was followed by a soft but distinct *thud.*

Harry smiled at McKenzie. "I guess we don't have to worry about Pat anymore. I'd be willing to bet he made it onto the boat."

* * * * *

Indeed, Nelson had made it onto the *Belle*, using a grappling hook and rope off the stern of the paddleboat to climb aboard. It hadn't been easy, and he was nearly out of breath when he thought a guard had spotted him, in spite of the dark clothing and the charcoal he had smeared on his face. But his fast thinking to use the grappling hook as a lasso worked, hitting the guard on the head. He dragged the man out of sight, then gagged and tied him up.

Now, crouching as close to the wall as he could, Pat waited for the right moment to take down a second guard, who seemed to be poking around, and when it came, he hit the man with his sap. The noise the second guard made when he hit the deck was faintly audible to McKenzie and Howser, though they couldn't identify the sound this time.

After dragging that body out of sight, Pat felt the man's neck for a pulse. He was still alive. The words of McKenzie—*Unless we are fired upon or attacked with deadly intent, I want to try to avoid killing anyone*—kept running through Nelson's head, because his military mind automatically told him these men were the enemy that must be destroyed.

Meanwhile, McKenzie and Harry strained their eyes to penetrate the growing darkness while they waited for the signal from Nelson that would let them know the forward boarding ramp was unprotected and they should board. They were about ready to go without the signal when Nelson appeared like a shadow at the top of one of the two boarding ramps and gave a come-on wave with his hand.

"Move, Harry," McKenzie whispered. "Be quick and quiet about it." He knew Nelson was watching out for them, but still he couldn't help but feel that there was a gun aimed right at them.

The two men boarded the *Southern Belle* cautiously, hearts pounding. Pat hustled them to cover, where they waited for several minutes, pinned against the wall, listening for any sign that they had been heard.

"It's this way," McKenzie instructed, pointing his cane once they were confident no guards were around. "Harry, you stay put and keep watch. Keep your ears open. Give out one of those bird calls of yours if you think that we've been discovered."

"Right," Harry grunted, drawing his recently manufactured Cooper double-action pistol from his shoulder holster.

"Remember, Harry," McKenzie said, looking down at the revolver. "Only as a last resort."

"Go," Harry whispered. "Get the boy"

McKenzie turned to Nelson. "Lead the way, Sergeant," he said quietly.

Nelson started back again, heading toward the stern of the boat. When they came to the stairway that would take them below decks, he paused. "Alicia said that from here, we'll be going down two more levels. I'll cover you on the first."

McKenzie nodded. They had already decided that while McKenzie guarded the stairs, Nelson would go through the cabin deck, clearing it of any obstacles, which in this case meant anyone he encountered.

The pair descended the stairs, where McKenzie stationed himself at the bottom while Nelson made his way down the narrow corridor of rooms. His pistol was out, but his finger was off the trigger to prevent an accidental discharge if something startled him. His free hand was on the sap in his pocket.

Once he felt certain that this level was clear, he walked back and signaled to McKenzie to follow him.

They had passed by all the staterooms and had made it to the end of the corridor when they were suddenly challenged from behind. A tall heavyset deckhand had rounded the corner, and, upon seeing the pair, had pulled a pistol from his belt.

"No need for that," McKenzie said, stepping forward to face the man. His body shielded Patrick's gun from view as he started walking toward the sailor. McKenzie acted nonchalant, allowing his cane to tap lightly on the floor.

"Relax. It's all right, Longwood sent us," he said, pasting a wide grin across his face.

"Yeah?" the man said suspiciously. "I didn't hear nothin' about no strangers showing up. So you stop right there."

"We're here about the boy," McKenzie said, stopping just out of the man's arm reach. "If Jason didn't send us, then how on earth would we know about the kid in the first place and where to find him?"

The man was thrown off by this question, not to mention McKenzie's friendly manner and his seemingly sensible explanation for being aboard the *Belle*. It made the man pause long enough for John to act.

McKenzie was not close enough to grab for the pistol, but since he didn't want it firing to alert any others on the boat, he wouldn't have tried anyway. Instead, he twisted his wrist clockwise, sending the shaft of his solid teak wood cane flying upward in a half circle. The cane hit the outside of the man's right hand, breaking several bones in his wrist. The gun dropped and slid out of reach.

Without any hesitation, McKenzie continued the cane's trajectory in a reverse figure eight, drumming it down hard on the man's neck right over the jugular notch. The man crumbled to the floor.

After an attempt to open a cabin door using the knob, Nelson hammered the door open with a few hard kicks. The pair dragged the man inside, where McKenzie gagged and tied him up as fast as he could with shaking hands.

"Think anyone heard us?" McKenzie asked.

Nelson shook his head. "They would have had to be pretty close to hear. If they did, they'd be here by now, wouldn't they?"

"Maybe," McKenzie replied grimly.

"Alicia said there wasn't another guard until she came to the end of the next deck," Nelson reminded McKenzie, even though he knew John had a mind like a steel trap for details when on a mission.

"Yeah, well, she didn't see anyone else on this deck either," McKenzie muttered under his breath, but Nelson heard him.

"Remember, it's said a battle plan goes right out the door once the first shot is fired, and a shot hasn't been fired . . ." Patrick said, but he was cut off.

"Yet, Pat, not yet. Let's hope we can keep it that way until we find Andy. Let's also hope that Harry is all right," McKenzie said, then paused to listen for movement coming from any direction. When he felt assured that they hadn't been heard, he nudged Nelson, saying: "You go first, Pat. Let's go find Andy."

"Yes, sir."

The pair descended the stairs quietly, and once at the bottom, they switched positions. McKenzie paused to straighten his coat and tie. He lowered his broad-brimmed hat down over his face, and took a deep breath.

The idea was that in the poor light, McKenzie would be confused for Jason Longwood because of their similar height and build and mustache.

Once they had crossed the empty cargo deck and approached

the stairway, they saw a guard stationed there. A chain strung across the entry prohibited access.

When they were within hearing distance of the guard, Patrick began a conversation as though their presence was nothing out of the ordinary.

"I don't know, Mr. Longwood, do you think it's a good idea to check on the boy at this hour? He's probably sleeping."

Upon hearing his boss's name, the guard quickly pulled back his shoulders, looking straight ahead as if in the military. His eyes tried to focus on the faces of the two men, but in the dim light, he couldn't be sure who either was, even though the taller resembled Jason Longwood.

As the pair approached, the guard realized neither was Longwood. Not knowing what to do when he saw the smaller man brandishing a gun at him, he stood in place, almost frozen, his lips attempting to form words but unable to do so. The guard turned his head as if looking for someone to come to his aid.

Nelson worked in closer, and, when he was in range, he hit the man in the head with his sap. Before the man could react, the force of that blow snapped his neck back. When Nelson hit him again, he fell forward, landing straddled over the chain precariously.

The pair of detectives quickly moved his body over near a pile of gunnysacks, where they covered him with empty bags.

"I got the impression he was trying to warn someone . . . maybe down below," McKenzie whispered. "I think there's at least one more guard."

"Never really thought there wouldn't be," Pat replied with a slight grin, though his focus remained on the bottom of the stairwell. He thrived on the threat of danger once he was in battle.

"Small change of plans, Pat," McKenzie whispered. "Once we get to the bottom step, you stay there unless I need you . . . and that will be my call, not yours.

"I don't like that idea," Nelson said quietly.

"It's an order, Sergeant," McKenzie said. "We need to appear nonthreatening. The last thing we want to do is to alarm the guard."

"You're assuming there's only one guard down there. What if there are more?" Nelson pointed out in a whisper.

"That's precisely why I'm going in alone. If I get in a bind, you'll be nearby."

That was it.

McKenzie slipped down the stairs, not encountering anyone. He glanced at his watch before carefully opening the door and peeking into the engine room. He stepped inside, recalling the layout of the boat he had reviewed over and over again. He walked at a relaxed pace until he reached the storage room Jimmy had pointed out. A guard was posted there. This one was almost twice the size of the previous man, and he looked like he ate anvils for dinner. In spite of his size, however, the guard was agile and moved fast. Before McKenzie knew it, a sawed-off shotgun appeared out of nowhere and was leveled right at his midsection.

"Whoa there, big hoss, I'm unarmed. More importantly, I'm on your side," McKenzie said, forcing a smile and raising his hands above his head.

"Yeah, well, my pap raised me up not to trust nobody," the man said.

Very slowly and very carefully, McKenzie lowered his arms, opening and displaying the interior of his coat to the guard. He had a gun hidden in his coat pocket, but by holding the sides out he hoped the guard wouldn't bother with the pockets.

"See . . . no weapons. Jason said I was to come unarmed. I already explained that to the other fellow up above," he said, a nod of his head to indicate the direction of the stairway.

The guard took a step forward and shoved the shotgun

barrel deep into McKenzie's midriff, hitting a couple of ribs hard, as he patted down his sides with his free hand. He found no weapons on the detective.

"What are you doing here?" the guard asked, taking a step back and remaining suspicious. "And who the hell are you?"

"A colleague and financial backer of Jason's, if you must know. I'm aware that the actress lady, what's her name . . . Edwards, that's it . . . takes care of the boy during the day, but Jason . . . Mr. Longwood to you . . . still has backers with some last-minute concerns. That's why they sent me to check on the status of the lad."

The guard cocked his head in disbelief.

"I know you don't believe me, but ask yourself what else I'd be doing here at night, unarmed, with somebody poking a double-barrel in my gut?"

"Well, you are making sense, but . . ." The man stopped, not totally convinced. "I didn't hear nothing about it though."

"I'm sorry about that. Don't you go to the meetings . . . or aren't you invited?" McKenzie asked sarcastically, grasping at straws and so far winning.

As expected, the man appeared insulted by what McKenzie was insinuating.

Before the guard could ask any more questions, McKenzie politely removed his hat, shifting his cane to his right hand. He knew that after belittling the man, he had to build him up again to get him on his side.

"You obviously were the right man for this job. The boy couldn't be guarded by anyone more qualified. I'll be certain to let the men I work with know all about you," McKenzie stated, which seemed to relax the guard somewhat. But McKenzie kept on, after letting out a loud sigh of relief. "My . . . but you did give me a start though," he said with a laugh. "What's your name?"

The burly guard chuckled, lowering his shotgun as he said: "Fred Knowles."

"So, Fred, can I just take a quick look at the boy?" McKenzie asked.

"I guess it's all right," Knowles replied. "Not much you could do anyway without a weapon." He gestured toward the cabin door. "The kid's in there. Checked up on him not that long ago . . . sleeping like a baby."

"And he's alone now, right?" McKenzie asked, praying he hadn't overstepped.

"Like you said yourself, that Edwards lady works here during the day . . . cooks for him, plays with him. She left about two hours ago. No need for anyone else besides me at this time of night," the man said proudly.

Now that the guard was no longer suspicious, McKenzie said: "Thanks. I needed to know that for sure, and I truly am sorry."

Knowles looked at him as though he were crazy. "Sorry . . . for what?" he asked.

"This," McKenzie said calmly as he flourished his cane and ran the tip of it into the man's stomach.

Fred Knowles's eyes stayed on McKenzie, a look of astonishment on his face as he grabbed his midsection and dropped to his knees.

"For having done that, you kidnapping son of a bitch," McKenzie replied, waiting patiently to make sure no one else was around to have heard his conversation with Knowles.

One minute.

Two minutes.

He pulled out his pistol, prepared to use it as he opened the cabin door, keeping his head outside as he listened one last time for the sound of footsteps. Then he stepped into the dark room. It took time for his eyes to adjust to a further diminishment of light. But slowly the small room and its contents took shape as he scanned the room from left to right. To his relief, he saw Andy asleep on a narrow bed, covers drawn up to his chin.

Without even thinking, McKenzie scooped him up, blanket and all, grabbed his clothes from the foot of the bed, not knowing if they were the ones from the photo or not, and backed out of the room, noting that the boy was light as a feather.

"John," a voice called out hoarsely.

McKenzie turned to see Pat moving toward him.

"I thought I heard something," Nelson said as he bent over, hands on knees, his breath coming in short gasps.

"Maybe you did. Where did the sound come from?" McKenzie asked, feeling another wave of relief even though the hardest part had yet to be accomplished, which was getting Andy off the boat. He looked down into the face of the sleeping boy, wondering if they had given him something to make him sleep, since he still slept soundly. *Not a concern now*, he told himself, *the boy is alive.*

He glanced around, saying: "You lead the way out, Pat. I'll follow behind with the boy. When we get to the second staircase, I'll stay back until you make sure it's clear."

"If we run into trouble . . . we . . . uh?" the ex-marine sergeant asked significantly.

"Take care of any of the bastards we encounter, if you must."

The two men slowly made their way up through the decks, stopping only once so McKenzie could shift his hold on the boy. But as he did so, the boy awakened.

"Who . . . who are you?" Andy asked as he strained his head back and stiffened, fear making his eyes wide.

"We're friends of your parents, Andy. Your grandpa sent us to get you away from these bad people and to take you back to your mother and father where you belong," McKenzie explained in hushed tones as he set Andy down on the floor. Now that he was standing, John could see that the boy was very small for his age.

"Really?" the boy asked, studying the two men suspiciously.

"Cross my heart and hope to die," Pat Nelson answered, looking into the lad's eyes. "But you have to be a brave little man while we're together. You keep quiet and do exactly what we tell you to do. Can you do that?"

"I think so," Andy answered, slowly bobbing his head.

"Quiet now and follow me," McKenzie said to the boy, taking his small hand in his own and guiding it to his coattail. "Hang on to my coat . . . don't let go," he instructed Andy. His derringer was leveled straight ahead. On Andy's right, Nelson watched the trio's rear. The two men acted as a shield as best they could.

Two men burst into view from around a corner at the far end of the hallway. McKenzie and Nelson fired simultaneously, dropping both men in their tracks. They knew the shots would be heard by anyone on the boat. That the shots had been loud was attested to by Andy, who stood with his hands clamped over his ears and tears filling his eyes.

"That'll draw somebody's attention for sure," McKenzie said, squatting and holding Andy to his torso in an effort to calm him. "We've got to hurry now, Pat."

Nelson nodded, looked back down the hall, and then snatched up the boy. He picked up the pace, letting McKenzie cover both ahead and behind them. They made it to the end of the hall and approached the staircase up to the next level. On the count of three, they made a mad dash up the stairs.

At the top of the stairs, McKenzie pulled the boy and his clothes from Nelson's arms and settled him next to a barrel, telling him to put his clothes on over his pajamas but to be quiet as a mouse. Nelson spotted Harry and waved him over, hoping he would see the gesture in the growing darkness. He did, slowly making his way over to the trio in a crouched position as the sound of activity seemed to be picking up from various quarters.

Harry squatted down by Andy, smiling as he did so.

"Andy, this man is your friend too," McKenzie told the boy. "His name is Harry. You can trust him, and you must do everything he says and stay close to him. You can do that, right?"

Again, Andy nodded his head and muttered: " I guess so."

McKenzie patted the boy's shoulder, saying: "Good boy." Then he turned to Harry. "Little change in plans," he said before the magician could get a word out. "I'm staying here to make sure we find every person involved in this kidnapping. I'm assuming the Pinks are out there, but in case . . . You know what you have to do, Harry."

Harry nodded and then smiled at the boy, promising to show him some magic tricks if he was really good and stayed close. Harry hugged the wall as he guided the boy toward the ramp that led down to the dock.

Less than ten feet from the ramp, Harry heard Andy trying to hold back his sobs, so he stopped and leaned down to talk to the boy. Andy said he was scared when Harry asked him what was wrong.

"There's nothing wrong with being scared, you just have to convince yourself that you're braver than you think you are," Harry told him. "I bet you were scared when those men took you."

Andy bobbed his head.

"But you were brave, and now you're going home. You just have to be brave for a little while longer. Can you do that, Andy?"

"Yes, yes I can," Andy replied.

"Good boy. Follow me," Harry said, and he scurried down to a spot in deep shadow almost directly across from the ramp.

"I want you to run over there. I'll be right behind you," Harry instructed, then turned the boy around. "Run!" he whispered in Andy's ear. He looked right and saw no one, but as he turned his head to the left, he saw a man headed his way out of the corner of his eye. But the man wasn't aiming at him, he was aiming at Andy.

"Hey, buddy!" he yelled to draw the man's attention. Then he was yelling at Andy to keep going, but he couldn't even look to see if the boy was running, because he had stepped out from the shadows and taken a couple of steps at the man with a shotgun aimed now at him.

Harry started to put his hands up, but he stopped moving them as his hands reached the top of his head where a bowler was perched. He removed his derby and held it flat against his chest with one hand, and with the other took his gun out from his pocket, using only his index finger and thumb, and placed it on the floor.

"Stop and listen to me," he said.

Surprising to Harry, the man stopped, and Harry took those first seconds to shoot the man with a .22-caliber bullet from the Sharps derringer affixed to the inside of his hat by two specially crafted metal clips. He had fired right through the top of his hat.

"That's for my having to ruin a perfectly good hat!" he hissed at the man, then ran to the ramp where he found Andy halfway down, standing, looking too petrified to move.

Now shouting could be heard coming from the boat.

Nelson knew that Harry and Andy were in grave danger if the crew started showering the two with bullets. He watched on tenterhooks as they made it to the bottom of the ramp and over to a trio of barrels twenty feet away from the water.

"Harry, keep going! We'll cover you! GO!" Nelson yelled, glancing over to see a group of men charging toward the head of the ramp. "Harry, run!"

McKenzie had moved over to Nelson's side. He edged even

closer, saying: "I'll keep an eye on Harry and the boy and cover them. You get ready to pick off anyone you can see holding a gun aimed at them," McKenzie told Nelson.

When two shots rang out from the upper deck—one directed at them that didn't even come close and one in the direction of Harry and the boy—McKenzie jumped out and sent several bullets in that direction. At the sound of a cry of pain from above, he smiled over at Nelson who gave him a nod of approval.

* * * * *

Three drunks weaved as they wandered around the dock, passing the barrels that hid Harry and Andy. They were singing at the same time Nelson was yelling at Harry to get a move on. When Nelson quit yelling, Andy told Harry he was ready to run again. Harry scanned the top deck of the boat, looking for any sign of men, but he didn't see a one, so he grabbed Andy's hand and they ran out from behind the barrels and past the drunks. They ran and ran, stopping whenever Andy needed to catch his breath. Harry knew they had to make the sharp right turn unseen and then get into the maze of crates designed by Harry and Jimmy and built by Marv Morgan and his men. He looked back when Andy slowed again, and that was when he saw maybe five or six men in pursuit.

"Stay right here, Andy," he gasped. "I promise I'll be right back."

Harry ran back to the drunks, talking so fast it was surprising they could understand him. They took the money Harry pushed at them and were busy counting it as he ran back to Andy.

"I heard somebody mention my name," Andy said the minute Harry was back, squatting beside him.

"It's all right. You're safe. We have to keep going, Andy. It's not far," Harry said as he got to his feet.

"There they are!" someone yelled.

"Hey, don' I know you from shomewhere," one of the drunks was saying to the pursuers. "Shure I do. Right . . ." Then all three were leaning into the pursuers, making it impossible for them to get through the boxes and barrels stacked around.

The words of one of the drunks seemed to drift away as Harry hustled Andy around the corner, and then he made a tight right turn, almost heading back the other way, and into a small entry between two boxes. Harry guided the boy through what seemed to someone under ten a mountain of boxes of all shapes and sizes from which they would never escape. Finally, Harry stopped in front of a large crate, which gave them a moment to listen to guns firing in a steady rhythm and the voices of those in pursuit.

"They've disappeared!" hollered one of the men.

"That's not possible, Joe!" answered another.

"Well, tell me where they are then," Joe yelled back.

"Spread out and find them!" yelled a new voice. "But stop your yapping!"

The group looking for Harry and Andy had swelled to ten or eleven men by now.

* * * * *

Some six minutes later, one of Longwood's men spotted Harry and the boy emerge from the opposite side of the maze. He gave a shout as he caught a glimpse of the two zigzagging between the cargo. He jumped up on one of the crates himself to keep the two in sight. He looked back to find the others, and when he swiveled back, he saw the boy and the man climbing into a buggy. The driver cracked his whip, and the buggy took off.

* * * * *

Suddenly the shooting came to a halt, and Longwood's men started shouting to each other, some from the *Belle* and others from the dock.

"Get the horses! Eight of 'em. The rest stay here and keep fighting."

It took a number of precious minutes for the eight men to get to the hitching rack where their horses were tied up. Near to the horses, a small explosive had been planted by Harry. He and Jimmy had rigged it as part of the "distraction" to be used when Harry and Andy were getting off the boat. But because the shooting started before they had a chance to get off the boat, it hadn't been detonated. However, McKenzie knew of its location, so he waited for the men to get closer.

He watched the men untether their horses from the rack. The animals were already jumpy from all of the shooting as the men started to mount up. That's when McKenzie shot the explosive. It went off on the third.

The horses began starfishing and bucking while the men struggled to stay on or get off their animal. The men were cursing their horses as they tried to bring them under control, because they were losing precious time.

* * * * *

Nelson and McKenzie returned fire whenever a bullet or two was fired their way. They determined they had to get off the steamboat. So when there seemed to be a lull in the shooting, they ran down the ramp, dodging left and right to avoid any sporadic gunfire. Upon reaching the dock, they scrambled to get to cover, finally pulling several barrels over to a pile of crates that they fashioned into a fort of sorts. Once they settled in, they realized that from their new position, they could stop anyone from going up or coming down either of the *Southern Belle*'s ramps.

They counted at least six men firing at them from the deck, and when one of them attempted to charge down a ramp, he was stopped by a bullet.

"We should have stashed a couple of rifles on the dock beforehand," McKenzie commented to Nelson while reloading his handgun.

"I'll try to remember that for next time. If there is a next time, that is," Pat mumbled.

The gunfire was picking up again when suddenly Nelson fired two shots and lunged toward McKenzie, shoving him to the ground. "Look out, John!" he cried, having caught only a glance at two men sneaking up on them. He had injured at least one of the men based on the grunt of pain he heard. At the sound of retreating footsteps going in the opposite direction, he slumped down at McKenzie's side.

The chief detective swore under his breath when he felt the warm blood oozing from Nelson's shoulder. He jumped up in anger and fired his pistol at a man running in the opposite direction.

"I got one, Pat," he said, his breath coming hard. "How bad is it?"

"Hurts like hell," Nelson replied, and he let out a slight groan before shifting his body. "I'll live."

McKenzie pulled his friend up to a sitting position, his back pressed against the splintery wood of the box, and said: "What say we both live?"

A shot rang out from the boat, chipping away a piece of wood from the box right in front of McKenzie.

"Well, we'll live if those reinforcements get here in time,"

McKenzie said, then began loading the empty chambers of his pistol. "But until there's some sign of them, do you think you can shoot?"

"Got me in the left shoulder, John. I shoot with the right, remember?" With that he picked up his gun and returned fire when a bullet clunked in the ground nearby. "You'll have to help me reload though," he informed McKenzie.

"All right, but switch pistols with me. I just reloaded. Keep them busy, if need be, while I reload your gun."

* * * * *

For the next ten minutes, the two managed to prevent any attempt to escape off the boat, as well as repelled a second attack from the dock. Still, they were just as pinned down and trapped as were the men on the boat.

"I don't know how long we can hold off these men, Pat. How many rounds have you got left?"

"About twenty more," Nelson replied.

McKenzie checked his coat pockets where he'd stashed some extra rounds for his pistol. They hadn't been discovered by the guard.

"I've got thirty rounds left," McKenzie said, a waver of concern in his voice.

Nelson laughed. "Yeah, but my balls are bigger," he said, referring to the .36-caliber lead ball ammo used in his Navy Colt. Coming from the marine sergeant, it was pretty good joke.

McKenzie chuckled despite their bleak supply of ammunition. "You know, we're probably fighting off seasoned soldiers or sailors. Could be some veterans among them."

Nelson was about to disagree, but he stopped to listen while trying to see out a small space between two crates. He could make out men moving about on the boat. He watched for a minute more before he understood what they were doing.

Nelson slid back down and gave McKenzie a meaningful look. "I think they're going to rush us . . . use both ramps to get off the boat, knowing we can't possibly get them all in the fading light, especially if they keep a steady barrage coming our way."

McKenzie nodded in reply, not certain if Nelson even saw him do it. He eased up to get a look himself if he could. Shapes were hardly discernable in the shadows.

"Let's make these bullets count," McKenzie said to Nelson.

The two prepared themselves to put up a fight that both judged to be hopeless. Neither said anything.

Each man was thinking his own thoughts as they sat there, but ready to go when McKenzie gave the word. Just as he was about to give the order, the sound of horses approaching fast could be heard.

Nelson let his gun hand drop so that he could cradle his wounded shoulder as he shifted. He let out a sigh, then smiled to himself weakly, before he said: "Captain, looks like that relief you were hoping for arrived just in the nick of time."

McKenzie let himself relax momentarily for the first time in what seemed like hours.

* * * * *

The posse that Pinkerton had put together numbered twenty-two men, made up of five Pinkertons, nine local lawmen, and eight cowboys from Schurz's ranch. They quickly dismounted, split up into groups, then started trading shots as they inched closer to the boat. The firepower alone was enough to drive the men on the boat into hiding, and in what seemed like a matter of minutes, the Pinks and the lawmen moved up the ramps and boarded the *Southern Belle.*

Longwood's men didn't need much convincing that they

were outnumbered and outgunned, and by ones and twos they surrendered.

Nelson was sitting on a crate not far from where he had been shot, holding a wadded handkerchief to his wound. McKenzie stood near him, alternating between staring at the boat and the water.

Allan Pinkerton hurried over to them. "You got the boy, right? He wasn't hurt?"

"I'm good, sir," McKenzie said in reply. "Thanks for asking. Pat, however, will need a doctor to tend to his shoulder.

"Yes, yes of course," Allan answered almost before McKenzie had finished. "But the boy, John, the boy? Where is he?"

CHAPTER EIGHTEEN

The covered buggy with two passengers was being pursued by eight of Longwood's men. Although the "distraction" had delayed their pursuit, they had made up time by pushing their horses. And they had the buggy in their sight now. But then again, part of the plan was having them follow the carriage, just not too closely.

"It might be getting dark, but it ain't that dark that we can't follow that buggy," said one of the mounted men in the lead.

"They ain't gonna lose us," another rider responded. "We'll get the kid back."

About a mile out of town, the riders began to close in, and to their surprise, the buggy started to slow as they neared a well-known but out-of-the-way roadside tavern. Even in the fading light, it was evident that the wood building was badly in need of paint, although the sign that read MCGUINTY'S PUB. RUM AND BEER AVAILABLE looked to have been refreshed recently.

"We got 'em now!" a rider toward the back shouted in triumph. "One of 'em horses musta played out."

The fellow in the lead called out: "Circle 'round 'em before they get down out of that damned rig!"

The riders pulled back on their reins as the buggy came to a full stop in front of McGuinty's, but they approached it cautiously, not knowing what to expect next. When nothing happened, they circled their horses around the carriage.

The looks on their faces when, from the driver's seat, Jimmy Piper tapped the rim of his hat as he looked first ahead, then to one side and the other.

"How can we help you fellows?" he asked innocently, once he had let six of the men get a good look at his youthful face.

"What the hell?" a slim rider asked, getting down from his horse and drawing his gun while keeping an eye on Jimmy. "You're just a boy yourself," he said.

"Boy?" The word echoed from inside the buggy. "You men surely wouldn't be referring to me now, would you?" Mickey asked angrily, throwing open the door and placing his cigar in the corner of his mouth so he could steady himself before climbing down.

"I'll be damned. It's a midget!" a rider exclaimed, and then he couldn't help it, he started laughing.

"Quite astute of you," Harry said as he climbed out of the buggy. "But my friend here prefers the term 'short gentleman.'"

A rider wearing a beat-up straw hat leveled his gun at Harry. "I saw you running down the dock. You and the kid both was as plain as day to me."

"So you're saying that, in the dark, you thought my friend here was a child?" Harry inquired, a smirk on his lips.

"Wait a second," another rider said, coming over by Harry and Mickey from the other side. "He's dressed just like that there kid was, Slim."

"I don't know who you men are referring to, but I'll have you know I purchased my attire at a reputable store in Chicago. Though to be honest, I admit that I wear the clothing of children at times . . . saves on the altering costs, you see," Mickey said, puffing his cigar the whole while he spoke.

The men at the back side of the buggy moved around to have a look.

"Tell me, just who is this boy you mentioned . . . the one you are apparently looking for?" Harry asked.

"None o' your business," the one with the straw hat said angrily.

"Say, what were you two doing on the dock, anyway?" Slim asked.

Harry sighed before answering. "Not that it's any of your business, as one of your men so rudely pointed out, but since we're clearly at a disadvantage here . . . you fellows waving your guns about . . . I'll tell you. See, we were supposed to meet up with a pair of ladies that we met in one of the drinking establishments . . .

"Yeah, so then why'd you take off running?" Slim butted in to ask.

"You mean back there on the dock?" Mickey asked innocently, puffing so hard on his cigar that his head seemed to be encased in a cloud. "Well, when we heard gunshots, we naturally thought it was them ladies' husbands firing at us. Be damned if we was going to hang around long enough to find out."

"If you'll excuse me for interrupting," Harry said, taking a step closer to the fellow called Slim. "Might I venture to say the boy you are looking for could still be back there on that dock? We heard a lot of shooting going on when we were heading out of town."

Several of the riders looked at each other, wondering what they should do next. Harry had given them something to think about.

"So, what now?" the man with the straw hat asked of no one in particular. "Do we leave them go, or take 'em back to Long— or take care of them here and now?" The man looked at Slim, knowing he had said too much.

Jimmy Piper turned around to get a good look at the men. "If I might make a suggestion, gentlemen," he said. "Shooting these two men will only result in great personal harm to each and every one of you. Fatal in fact. So, I would . . ."

"Yeah, sure, kid? You gonna protect them yourself?" one of the riders asked with a laugh. Several of the men laughed with him. "But what I want to know is, what makes you think we wouldn't kill you right along with them?"

Jimmy nodded his head as if considering the question. After a good long pause, he cocked his head in the direction of the tavern. "Me, stop you . . . oh, no," he said with a smile, then jumped down off the driver's seat, adding: "No, definitely not me, but you should know there are half a dozen carbines pointing at you from inside McGuinty's."

Heads turned to look at the sun-bleached building. A curtain covering a window was pulled back from the inside to reveal the barrels of two rifles aimed in the direction of the carriage and the men around it.

"And if you men will look over to your left," Harry added, "you will see a few more men hidden out there among the trees and bushes. No matter the number, since they are all reputed to be very good shots."

"And at this distance even I couldn't miss," Mickey added, pointing his cigar at one of the men like a pistol.

"So, I'd advise you to drop your weapons, boys," Harry said, flashing a grin at them. "It's better to be arrested as highwaymen than shot dead as conspirators and kidnappers. Of course, you could try to make a run for it, but I suspect the chance of your surviving long as free men would be short-lived."

At a signal from Harry, the men among the trees stood up, cocking their rifles as they did so. After a few tense moments in which Jimmy, Harry, and Mickey could have easily been caught in the crossfire, Longwood's men began surrendering their weapons and putting their arms in the air.

* * * * *

Having seen that one of the Pinks had been hit in the shoulder, several cowboys from Senator Schurz's ranch were rigging a stretcher out of blankets they found aboard the *Southern Belle* and two long-handled brooms. When they came over with it and tried to assist him onto it, Pat pushed away from the men, insisting he was fine and only in need of directions to a good doctor.

"I can still walk, dammit!" he protested when the cowboys looked like they were ready to strong-arm him onto the stretcher.

John McKenzie saw what was going on and walked over. "You've lost a fair amount of blood, Patrick. You might get dizzy walking too far. I can't afford to lose you, you know. So just get on the stretcher."

"I'd rather not, John," Pat said. It was obvious he was both angered and embarrassed by all the attention.

"But as your boss, *I* sure as hell can order you to get on that stretcher," Allan Pinkerton said, stepping forward. "Now lay your ass down, and we'll take you to a doctor, Sergeant Nelson!"

"Yes, sir," he said, giving both Allan Pinkerton and McKenzie a look as he eased down onto the makeshift travois.

CHAPTER NINETEEN

Alicia Faye was standing at the end of the dock, far away from the *Southern Belle* so that she would not be seen by McKenzie, who had ordered her to keep away. She had spent most of the day in a frazzle, trying to find Jason Longwood in order to keep him away from his steamboat. But no matter where she went, she seemed to have missed his departure by only minutes. By late afternoon she knew he was playing a game with her, but she wasn't sure if he knew her true mission.

She arrived near the dock after seven thirty as the sky began to darken, earlier than usual with a storm threatening once again. The sound of gunfire was intermittent now. She tried to wend her way through all the people who were arriving to see what was going on. A deputy stopped her and told her to head back, that there was nothing to see. She thanked him, wishing as she did so that she had brought along her opera glasses to get a better look at what was going on nearer to the *Southern Belle*.

In spite of the lawman's warning, when she saw someone being lifted up on a stretcher, her heart started beating so fast and loud, she swore she could hear it. She picked up the hem of her dress in both hands and began walking toward the *Belle*, gaining speed with each step.

"Please, Lord, don't let it be John," she murmured over and over again.

She ran headlong into a group of men talking and tried to get past them, but was stopped from behind by a hand clamping across her mouth. Chills ran through her from the wet and cold clothes of the person pressing her back against him and pulling her backward, causing her to drop her reticule in which she carried her derringer.

A familiar voice whispered in her ear: "Alicia, what a surprise."

Jason Longwood!

Because he was soaking wet, she guessed he had been on the *Southern Belle* while she had combed the city, looking for him. And when things got difficult on the boat, the coward had jumped off.

"What am I to think . . . you looking for me all day long and then you turning up here?" Longwood asked.

Careful, Alicia, careful, she told herself, and then words came tumbling out. "Yes, I was looking for you today because . . . because I wanted to see you. When I heard all the shooting and people heading down here, I . . ."

"Be careful what you say, my dear. You see, I'm a man who doesn't believe in coincidences, and remember . . . I am well aware of your abilities as an actress." Then Longwood spun her around roughly so he could look her in the eye. "In fact, now that I think about it, it wouldn't surprise me if the famous Queen of the South has been in on rescue. That would be too bad. The ransom money might have helped the South, Alicia."

"More likely it would have gone into your personal coffers," Alicia snapped back.

"So you were spying on me all along, were you?" he said.

His jaw jutted forward, and his brown eyes looked dark and evil, as if they were stabbing into her and reading her thoughts. She decided not to say anything, believing that now anything she would say would only make things worse . . . because he was deranged.

"Well, at least you're smart enough not to deny it," he said when she said nothing. "But I am sorry it had to come to this."

He pulled her close and steered her through the gathering people till they came to an alley. He shoved her into it. Longwood studied her silently for several minutes, and then he started walking toward her, as she reached behind to feel for anything that could get in her way as she moved back. He kept coming and coming toward her, finally forcing her against the wall where he reached up and gently put his hands around her throat. His intentions were perfectly clear. He smiled as if he were enjoying the look of fear in her eyes, his grip becoming tighter, his fingers digging in.

It seemed like the air was taking form and moving around her head as he pressed harder. She knew she had to fight back, but the derringer was gone, somewhere on the ground where Longwood had grabbed her. The knife kept in her garter was impossible to reach with Longwood's weight on her, pushing her so that her backbone ground against the rough building bricks as he squeezed. But hanging from a lanyard at her wrist was the fan John had given her.

Alicia tightened her grip on the lanyard, her fingers pulling the fan within reach of her grasp in the tiniest of increments so Longwood wouldn't notice. She returned his stare now, trying to bore into the crazy man's mind how much she detested him. Then the fan was in her hand. She flicked it open and thrust it as hard as he could into Longwood, digging in under the breastbone in the area of his solar plexus.

He looked at her, disbelief in his eyes.

“I have one question,” Alicia said. “How did you know about the secret passageway at the hotel?”

Longwood’s lips curled up. “Oh, that. I’m sorry you don’t have time for the whole story. But I’ll tell you that I had a mother who was more interested in saving those darkies than she ever was in raising me . . . her only son. She had quite a little business going, saving those half-humans.”

Longwood couldn’t catch his breath nor could he maintain his grip on Alicia’s neck. He staggered back, his eyes still obsidian but no longer able to focus. As he stood there, his hand trying to hold in the blood soaking his shirt, his legs losing their strength, Alicia watched.

“I’m not sorry about this, Jason,” she whispered as she swiped the open fan along his throat.

It was the death blow for Jason Longwood. His heart, if he had one, stopped beating as he lay on the cobbles.

Alicia snapped the fan closed without thinking, an automatic response. But the shock of what she had just done started to make the alley feel as though it was closing in on her. Sweat glistened on her face as she made her way out of the alley on shaky legs, where she found a barrel to lean against.

Alicia stayed there for a number of minutes, concentrating on getting her breathing under control and the sweating to stop. Slowly, her heart settled into a normal rhythm and her breathing changed from shallow to deep. When she felt as though she had regained her composure, she stood up and began walking toward the *Southern Belle.*

* * * * *

“Is Alicia safe, Allan?” McKenzie asked, turning back to face his boss. He was concerned about her as usual.

"She should be," Allan replied. "When I spotted her a while back, I had one of the local lawmen order her to stay back from the dock where she'd be out of harm's way. Figured it was better coming from him than me."

"Don't you know it," McKenzie agreed with a slight chuckle. "I . . ."

"The Queen of the South is just fine," Alicia said, having steeled herself to come up to the two when she saw them talking in the midst of a sea of people.

At sight of her, McKenzie tried to hide the relief he felt from Allan.

As the two men turned to face Alicia, a man approached from the other direction, panting: "No sign of him, Mr. Pinkerton. At least none who fit the description you gave us." He was referring to Jason Longwood, of course.

"Dammit," McKenzie said angrily. "I wish I knew where he was hiding."

"If you're talking about Jason, he's in the alley right over there," Alicia reported, feeling an odd sense of euphoria at seeing John alive and unscathed while Longwood was gone for good.

"How . . . what . . .?" McKenzie tried to get out.

"He must have been on the *Belle* most of the day," she explained. "I tried to find him, but I think for a time he was playing cat and mouse with me. Anyway, he was soaking wet when he found me a while ago, so that's why I think he was on the boat and that he jumped off to save himself. He came up to me right over there." She waved her arm.

Immediately, Allan called over to two of his men, telling them: "I need one of you to go find the local police and the other to find a couple more men and get over to that alley." He pointed, glancing at Alicia to get confirmation. "We've got information that Longwood . . ."

"No need to get more men, Allan. Longwood's not going anywhere," Alicia said. "He's dead."

If they had been surprised to find Alicia at the dock, they were downright shocked with what she had just told them. Neither man could bring himself to ask her any questions about what had happened.

"That's . . . um . . . good news," Allan managed to get out after a bit of stumbling over his words.

Then they watched as several Pinks began moving people out and away from the alley.

"John, what about the boy . . . What about Andy?" Alicia asked. "Is he with Harry?"

"No, Alicia, but rest assured, he is in safe hands," John told her.

"Where is he, then?" Allan asked, looking even more worried than he had when he arrived at the dock.

"Come this way with me," McKenzie instructed both Allan and Alicia, leading them over to the collection of crates and barrels that formed the maze.

He took them on the same path Harry and the boy had followed while escaping Longwood's men. He made the hard right turn, surprising them both as they followed him. When they were at the middle approximately, McKenzie stopped. He paused there in front of two crates turned sideways and shuffled between them. He finally stopped next to a crate of large dimensions, about six feet tall, just as wide, solidly built.

Allan Pinkerton looked around in frustration. "What's going on, John?" he asked as his eyes darted around all the crates surrounding them. "If Andy's not with Harry, then where the hell is he?"

McKenzie smiled. "Right in front of you, Allan." He glanced at Alicia, who had remained quiet; all he could think was that she looked beautiful. When she caught him looking at her, he winked and tapped four times with his cane on the wall of the wooden crate in front of them. In response, there were three quick raps and then a short pause followed by one loud knock.

"Now wait," McKenzie said. Slowly the whole side of the crate began to move, one side being pushed out while the other moved inward.

Corporal Alvin Jones stood inside at attention. Behind him, on the floor, Andy was just waking up, having slept through almost the entire battle.

McKenzie stepped inside and knelt down in from of Andy, which made the child recoil in fear; not surprising considering the ordeal he had been through since he had been kidnapped.

"It's all right, Andy," said Corporal Jones from behind John. "These are two of the men who played a big part in getting you away from these bad men today. Allan Pinkerton, I'd like to introduce you to Andy, one of the bravest young men I've ever had the privilege of knowing. And, Andy, this is the famous detective, Allan Pinkerton. He's a friend of your grandfather's, and he's going to make sure you get back to your family safely in just a little while."

Andy hesitated, glanced up at Alvin, who nodded, then politely said: "Thank you, sir . . . Mr. Pinkerton."

"It's good to meet you," Allan said, before turning to McKenzie. "We'll talk later, John. Right now, our priority is to get Andy back to his parents. Sound good to you, Andy?"

The boy's eyes filled with tears as he softly answered: "Oh, yes, sir." Then he walked over by Alvin.

Corporal Jones squatted down to give Andy a hug and tell him once again that he was a brave boy.

"Very well done, Jones," Pinkerton commended the corporal as he stood back up. "Very well done, indeed." Then Allan took the soldier's hand and shook it.

"My honor, sir," the soldier replied, smiling widely.

Allan motioned to the little boy. "Let's go, Andy. It won't be long now before you're back with your family."

Having stayed on the sidelines, Alicia stepped forward and squatted in front of the boy. "You're safe now," she told him reassuringly. "Your parents are waiting." She leaned in to give him a kiss on the cheek.

With that, Allan took Andy to his personal carriage, and the two left the dock accompanied by several well-armed agents.

McKenzie looked at Alicia, and the two spontaneously hugged each other. They left the maze and stopped once out in the open again.

"I was so worried when I saw the stretcher," Alicia said, "thinking it was you, but then Longwood showed up . . ." She was too exhausted and embarrassed to go on.

"It was Pat who took a round in the shoulder, but he should be fine with a little time off. Something we could all use," McKenzie admitted.

"Thank God this is over, John," Alicia said, highly emotional at the moment. Suddenly she couldn't help herself, and she unexpectedly—to herself as well as John—kissed her boss tenderly on the lips, slipping her arms around his waist and crying uncontrollably.

"I hope we aren't interrupting anything important here," a familiar voice called out loudly from behind.

"Of course you are, Harry," Alicia said, sniffing and wiping the tears from her eyes as she backed away from John.

"Everything go all right at your end?" McKenzie asked Harry.

"Smooth as silk, John. The professor captured the whole group single-handedly while Mickey and I enjoyed a pint of ale in the pub."

"Oh, go on with you all," Jimmy said, having overheard.

He turned red as a beet when they all looked at him. “Seriously, boss,” he informed McKenzie, “everything went as planned. The men who followed us are no doubt sitting in a cell by now.”

“Wonderful!” McKenzie exclaimed. “In that case, Alicia and I will be heading back to the hotel in the carriage, and I suggest the rest of you head out for a round of drinks you deserve.”

CHAPTER TWENTY

It was almost a full week later that McKenzie, Nelson, Harry, and Alicia assembled at Allan Pinkerton's private office in Chicago. Three people were absent: Corporal Alvin Jones, who had returned to his unit; Mickey Dunn, who was back in St. Louis, trying out new tricks; and Professor Jimmy Piper, who had returned to his life as a scientist, carrying out experiments and occasionally teaching classes.

"How's the shoulder, Pat?" Pinkerton asked.

Nelson's arm was still in a sling. "Seems to be healing fine," he replied. "It turned out to be a clean through and through shot, just like I thought. More of a bother now than a pain. I'll live. Thanks for asking."

"Howser, I have to say, that crate idea you came up with was an inspiration," the head of the Pinkertons remarked, turning his attention to a small replica Harry had sent to him for demonstration purposes, which was now sitting atop his desk.

"It's a simple locked-door illusion," Harry explained, looking down at the replica. "Mickey and I perfected it over the years. See here," he said, pointing at the side of the box. "Instead of having the side open and close using hinges, which would be typical, this crate has a long bar that runs straight down the middle of the wooden panel, which allows the whole panel to turn three hundred and sixty degrees. It can be locked in position from the inside. Seen from the outside, the wall of the crate appears to be a normal closed panel that has been nailed shut." Harry straightened up and remained quiet while Pinkerton worked the tiny secret door. "Mind you, Mr. Pinkerton, a magician is never supposed to reveal his tricks."

Pinkerton laughed loudly. "I promise you, Harry, it will never go beyond this office. Right?" He eyed McKenzie, Nelson, and Alicia, and then settled on Harry.

"So, the way it worked was, Mickey Dunn was waiting inside the crate in the center of the maze with Alvin," Harry explained. "Mickey was a big help in knowing the right people down at the dock. They hauled in the prop and moved all the crates around to make room for the prop. Mickey cleverly marked our crate so I could find it easily, which was one of the reasons we had to do this when it was still light. So, no problem finding the magic box where inside, Mickey was dressed similarly to Andy in the photograph. I knocked like this"—Harry rapped on the desk—"and Mickey came out and Andy went in. So when I came running out with Mickey, Longwood's men saw us and were convinced they were still pursuing me and the boy. We magicians know that the eye sees what the brain wants it to. In a tight situation people don't notice the details. I had hoped that by dressing in a suit and bowler hat, and shielding the boy as we ran, any pursuers would be focused on me, being the larger of the two. It worked . . . the men chasing us expected to see me come out the other side of that maze of crates, dragging a small boy. And that's just what they saw. Classic sleight of hand.

"So as I said, Corporal Jones was in the crate with Andy,

who knew him from the hotel. But, boy, I'll tell you, Alvin was sure afraid that Andy wouldn't want to be locked up inside the box. On the other hand, I figured Andy was so used to being locked up in a small space by then, that being in the box didn't seem that different than being on the *Southern Belle*. And I was right, according to Alvin. Andy stayed calm through the whole ordeal." Harry paused briefly before adding: "That kid's got guts, that's for sure, just like his grandfather."

"Speaking of his grandfather, how did the reunion go?" Alicia asked. "I'm curious."

Allan smiled, saying: "I don't believe I've ever seen a happier group of people in my life. The senator . . . Andy's parents . . ."

"That's good to hear," McKenzie said as Allan leaned back in his chair. "And I don't know if you've heard, but Edith Edwards is spending six months in jail. She told us everything . . . more than we needed to know. She's willing to testify about the whole operation. She borrowed some money from Longwood to help pay off some gambling debts her father-in-law owed. Longwood offered to forgive the debt if she did a little job for him."

"That doesn't surprise me," Alicia said.

"Before I forget," Allan said. "The senator wanted me to express his gratitude to you all, since your work on this must remain more or less off the record. I assured him you would all be fine with that."

McKenzie nodded. "We are. That's not why we do the job. And, if there's nothing else for us to do here, sir . . . I'm sure Harry still has a few pockets to pick."

"Hey, not fair at all," Harry protested. "Both times I picked a pocket in St. Louis, it was just so I keep the old fingers nimble, you know. Besides, I found the fellows and gave them back the tips with a little extra, explaining how . . ."

"Sure, Harry, sure," Alicia interrupted.

"And the former Queen of the South?" Allan asked. "Any plans for starting up another show?"

Alicia blushed. "No, Allan, I don't have any. Actually, John and I thought perhaps we might take a small vacation."

Allan looked at McKenzie in time to see a look of embarrassment cross over his face. "Together?" Pinkerton asked, attempting to come across as being concerned.

Alicia looked over at John, hoping he would say something.

"Well, it's about time," Harry said when neither said anything.

McKenzie actually blushed at Harry's endorsement.

Pinkerton cleared his throat. "There is one last thing. I'm afraid a rather important case has just been given to the agency. An influential client with a problem." He paused, looking at McKenzie, before he asked: "Is there any way you can postpone this vacation a while?"

McKenzie looked over at Alicia and shrugged. She looked back at him and gave him a nod. "No rest for the restless, I guess," she said sweetly. "I'm in if you are."

"I'm available," Harry chimed in."

"Count me in," Nelson almost shouted. "But don't forget about that raise we discussed on the train, Captain."

John McKenzie surveyed the members of his team, let out a sigh, then, with a gleam in his eye, said to Pinkerton: "Fill us in."

AUTHOR'S NOTE

As I have written before, I grew up in the '50s and '60s, at a time when there were over fifty Westerns on prime-time television. The nighttime airwaves were filled with shows like *Gunsmoke*, *Bonanza*, *Bat Masterson*, and *The Rifleman*, just to mention a few. That was a remarkable number for one specific genre, especially when you consider that it doesn't include the daytime Western shows that were also being aired. Most of those were simply cutdowns of old pretelevision era Hopalong Cassidy movies and other Western serials of the '30s and '40s. Nevertheless, to a whole new audience of children, they were fun and exciting.

The popularity of Westerns wasn't just limited to the small screen. Disney Studios made movies like *The Tales of Davy Crockett*, *Westward Ho the Wagons!*, and *Old Yeller*, and they were all popular.

Of all these assorted Westerns, whether big screen or small, the one that most captured my attention was the now-iconic *The Wild Wild West*, starring Robert Conrad and Ross Martin. Each week, Secret Service agents James West and his partner Artemus Gordon ventured out into the western frontier to save the world. As a young boy, I desperately wanted to grow up to be just like James West.

Deep down inside, all of us who watched that series quickly realized that plastic explosives and much of the weaponry used on the show weren't really available in the 1800s, not to mention the fact that Secret Service agents back then didn't serve in spy missions like the ones West and Gordon were sent on. That fact didn't seem to matter to the viewing public, however, and the show quickly grew to become immensely popular. (One should also note that in several of its many episodes, the action actually took place in cities in the East.)

Another successful show from my youth was the television series *Mission: Impossible*. Every week viewers marveled as a specialized team of brave and creative modern-day spies solved national security problems by cleverly outwitting dangerous villains. The team came up with intriguing and ingenious solutions, and the series, just like the *The Wild Wild West*, combined adventure with creativity, good looks, brains, and brawn.

When I started writing Westerns, I had, in the back of my mind, the idea of someday combining these two iconic shows. I loved the courage, resourcefulness, and camaraderie of West and Gordon, and was excited by the concept of a team of government agents working together to solve a crime no one else could handle. (The beautiful women who appeared in each episode didn't hurt either.) Both shows coincidentally were full of clever disguises and tricky technology.

Out of this core idea came the outline for *No Rest for the Restless*. To this I added the Pinkertons. In the past I have written of the Texas Rangers, the Canadian Mounties, bounty hunters, and the US Cavalry. I believed, however, that no group of Western novels would be complete without including the now-iconic Pinkerton National Detective Agency.

That said, I freely acknowledge that there are many readers who believe Western literature should deal primarily with cowboys shooting it out in the street of a dusty town in Texas, or herding cattle to Abilene. On the other hand, I believe the West encompasses so much more. After all, half of that famous movie *How the West Was Won* occurred on the Erie Canal and Mississippi riverboats. Many Civil War stories, such as John Wayne's *The Horse Soldiers*, often took place back East, yet these are still considered by many to be Westerns in the traditional sense.

In *Bad Day at Black Rock*, actor Robert Ryan describes the West to Spencer Tracy by asking: "Which West?" He then speaks of the West of folklore, another of modern developers, still another of cattlemen, or of lawmen, and so much more. I feel the same way.

For me, a Western story should have certain well-defined characteristics, such as a clear cut difference between good and bad, a strong code of morality and bravery, a rugged sense of individuality, and a willingness for the hero or heroine to sacrifice themselves for the weak or innocent.

When I began to write this novel, I quickly realized that in order to follow a credible post–Civil War story line, the geographic setting had to take place farther to the East than the average Western town shoot-'em-up. The exact geographic location doesn't necessarily mean it should be excluded from the genre.

I had a lot of fun with the plot of *No Rest for the Restless* and sincerely hope the reader will too. As an aside, when an occasional anachronism pops up, be it a word, a term, or an activity, please go with the flow, as they say.

This book is meant to be an homage to the rather fantastic shows of my childhood. Even so, it is still coupled with much of the historical perspective of my earlier novels. At its core and in spirit, this story is meant to be a Western adventure to entertain the reader.

On a historical note, in 1847, a Scottish immigrant named Allan Pinkerton accidentally stumbled upon a band of counterfeiters and began what would turn out to be a very long and famous career as a detective. On his own, the young Scotsman conducted informal surveillance on the gang's activities, and then, after reporting what he had seen to the authorities, was hailed as a local hero for helping the police make their arrests. The affair was widely publicized, and Pinkerton found himself suddenly called upon to undertake other matters requiring his detective skills.

By the mid-1850s, businesses across the United States began to appreciate the need for more security and better control over their employees. They also recognized the importance of finding someone to investigate corporate fraud, theft, and corruption. Pinkerton, having become a full-time detective and part-time corporate spy, began to recognize the demand for such services. After consulting with the heads of six Midwestern railroads, he established an agency in 1855.

Pinkerton's organization was first established in Chicago, Illinois as the North-Western Police Agency. Formed as a private security guard and detective agency, it later became known by the name: the Pinkerton National Detective Agency.

Pinkerton later became even more famous when he claimed that his agents had foiled a plot to assassinate then President-elect Abraham Lincoln. Out of gratitude, Lincoln hired the Pinkerton Agency to handle the President's personal security during the Civil War. (At this point in history, the Secret Service had yet to be formed.)

Known among themselves—and to many outlaws—as "Pinks," Pinkerton's agents performed services during the war including security and bodyguarding, investigation, and political or military intelligence. At the height of its power, the Pinkerton National Detective Agency was the largest private law enforcement organization in the world.

In 1856, a twenty-three-year-old widow named Kate Warne walked into Pinkerton's Chicago office and requested a job as a detective. At first Pinkerton was hesitant to hire a female investigator for fieldwork. He finally consented after Warne convinced him that she could extract secrets in places where it might be impossible for male detectives to gain access.

Kate Warne became the first female private detective in American history and did such a good job that Pinkerton would later list her as one of the best investigators he had ever hired. Following Kate's death in 1868 and out of respect, Pinkerton had her buried in his own family's plot.

In later years, Pinkerton agents were hired to track Western outlaws such as Jesse James, the Reno Gang, and the famous Wild Bunch, headed up by Butch Cassidy and the Sundance Kid. Pinks also trailed and confronted the legendary Younger brothers and were instrumental in bringing the outlaws to justice.

Pinkerton agents were often hired to safeguard and transport money, as well as other high-quality merchandise between cities and towns. This, of course, made them somewhat vulnerable to outlaw attacks. Pinkerton agents, therefore, were usually well-trained, well-paid, and very well-armed.

More importantly, their dedication, integrity, intelligence, and persistence created a myth surrounding the agency. As the company's profile grew, its iconic logo, a large, unblinking eye, gave rise to the term "private eye" as a term for all detectives.

Their logo was later accompanied by the slogan "We Never Sleep." It was often said that there was no rest for a Pinkerton detective once he (or she) went out on the trail of an outlaw.

ABOUT THE AUTHOR

R. W. Stone inherited his love for Western adventure from his father, a former Army Air Corps armaments officer and horse enthusiast. He taught his son both to ride and shoot at a very early age. Many of those who grew up in the late 1950s and early 1960s remember it as a time before urban sprawl, when Westerns dominated both television and the cinema, and Stone began writing later in life in an attempt to recapture some of that past spirit he had enjoyed as a youth. In 1974 Stone graduated from the University of Illinois with honors in Animal Science. After living in Mexico for five years, he later graduated from the National Autonomous University's College of Veterinary Medicine and moved to Florida. Over the years he has served as President of the South Florida Veterinary Medical Association, the Lake County Veterinary Medical Association, and as executive secretary for three national veterinary organizations. Dr. Stone is currently the Chief of Staff of the Veterinary Trauma Center of Groveland, an advanced-level care facility. In addition to lecturing internationally, he is the author of over seventy scientific articles and a number of Westerns, including

Trail Hand (2006), *Badman's Pass* (2016), and *Across the Río Bravo* (2017). Still a firearms collector, horse enthusiast, and now a black-belt-ranked martial artist, R. W. Stone presently lives in Central Florida with his wife, two daughters, one horse, and three dogs.